# VOLUME THE THIRD

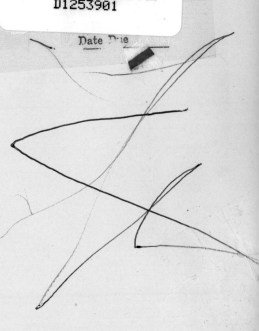

# VOLUME THE THIRD

BY

JANE AUSTEN

---

*Now first printed from
the Manuscript*

---

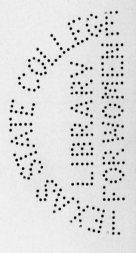

OXFORD
AT THE CLARENDON PRESS

---

MCMLI

*Oxford University Press, Amen House, London E.C.4*

GLASGOW NEW YORK TORONTO MELBOURNE WELLINGTON
BOMBAY CALCUTTA MADRAS CAPE TOWN

*Geoffrey Cumberlege, Publisher to the University*

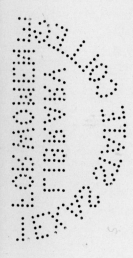

PRINTED IN GREAT BRITAIN

# PREFACE

Of Jane Austen's three volumes of juvenilia, 'Volume the Second' was published, as LOVE AND FREINDSHIP, by Messrs. Chatto and Windus in 1922, 'Volume the First' was published by the Oxford University Press in 1933. The series is now completed by 'Volume the Third', printed from the manuscript in the possession of Mr. R. A. Austen-Leigh.

This manuscript like its companions is (mainly) in Jane Austen's hand and is in a quarto volume. On the front cover she has written 'Volume the Third'. Inside the front cover someone has written in pencil 'Effusions of Fancy by a very Young Lady Consisting of Tales in a Style entirely new'.

On the first leaf J. A. has written 'Jane Austen—May 6th 1792' and

'Contents

Someone has added in pencil 'for James Edward Austen Leigh' (who did not become Leigh until 1837).

The manuscript ends on p. 127, a few blank leaves following. Its contents are briefly described in the *Life and Letters* by W. and R. A. Austen-Leigh (1913, p. 55).

Near the end (from 'Kitty continued', p. 125 of this reprint) a slight change in the hand, and a more obvious change in the colour of the ink, suggest that the last few pages were written later than the rest. This is confirmed by 'Mrs. Percival', which for the first time stands alone and is not an interlinear correction of 'Mrs. Peterson'. The conclusion may indeed be in a *different* hand; if so, it has not been identified.

Many of the pieces that make up the three volumes are dated, and the dates are not in chronological sequence. It is clear that the volumes are a collected edition of the author's works up to June 1793. They must have been transcribed from lost originals. There is, however, evidence of revision. Thus in Vol. III 'Kitty' is in several places changed to 'Catherine'; 'Peterson' is improved to 'Percival'; passages are erased.

The fragment called 'Kitty' (later promoted to 'Catherine') 'or the Bower' is unique among these juvenile effusions; in spite of the absurd dedication, this is Jane Austen's first essay in serious fiction. The authors of the *Life and Letters*,[1] who quote from the manuscript, point out that the story of the elder Wynne girl[2] is drawn from life: it describes, with some exaggeration, the fate of J. A.'s own aunt

[1] Pp. 31–4.        [2] *Infra*, pp. 34, 55.

Philadelphia Austen, who was shipped
to Madras in 1752 and became Mrs.
Hancock within seven months. Her
daughter Eliza, who became the Com-
tesse de Feuillide, lost her husband
by the guillotine in 1794, and became
Mrs. Henry Austen in 1797, paid a
visit to Steventon in 1792, the year in
which 'Catherine' was dedicated.

Loosely inserted in the book are
three leaves of manuscript signed
J. E. A. L. That is Jane Anna Elizabeth Lefroy, always known as Anna;
she was J. A.'s eldest niece, born 1793,
the daughter of her eldest brother
James by his first wife and half-sister
of James Edward, who became the
owner of the volume. Anna married
Benjamin Lefroy. Her attempts at
fiction are otherwise known to us from
her aunt's letters about them written
in 1814. The present fragment is her
contribution to 'Evelyn'.

R. W. C.

VOLUME THE THIRD

*Jane Austen—May 6th* 1792.

## CONTENTS

*To*

To Miss Mary Lloyd,

The following Novel is by permission
Dedicated,
by her Obed[t] humble Serv[t]

The Author

EVELYN

# EVELYN

In a retired part of the County of Sussex there is a village (for what I know to the contrary) called Evelyn, perhaps one of the most beautiful spots in the south of England. A Gentleman passing through it on horseback about twenty years ago, was so entirely of my opinion in this respect, that he put up at the little Alehouse in it & enquired with great earnestness whether there were any house to be lett in the Parish. The Landlady, who as well as every one else in Evelyn was remarkably amiable, shook her head at this question, but seemed unwilling to give him any answer. He could not bear this uncertainty—yet knew not how to obtain the information he desired. To repeat a question which had already appear'd to make the good woman uneasy was impossible—. He turned from her in visible agitation. "What a situation am I in!" said he

to

to himself as he walked to the window and
threw up the sash. He found himself revived
by the Air, which he felt to a much greater
degree when he had opened the window than
he had done before. Yet it was but for a
moment—. The agonizing pain[1] of Doubt &
Suspence again weighed down his Spirits.
The good woman who had watched in eager
silence every turn of his Countenance with
that benevolence which characterizes the
inhabitants of Evelyn, intreated him to tell
her the cause of his uneasiness. "Is there
anything Sir in my power to do that may
releive your Greifs—Tell me in what manner
I can sooth them, & beleive me that the
freindly balm of Comfort and Assistance
shall not be wanting; for indeed Sir I have
a simpathetic Soul."

"Amiable Woman (said M$^r$ Gower, affected
almost to tears by this generous offer) This
Greatness of mind in one to whom I am
almost a Stranger, serves but to make me
the more warmly wish for a house in this

[1] idea *erased.*

sweet

sweet village——. What would I not give to be your Neighbour, to be blessed with your Acquaintance, and with the farther knowledge of your virtues! Oh! with what pleasure would I form myself by such an example! Tell me then, best of Women, is there no possibility ?—I cannot speak—You know my meaning——."

"Alas! Sir, replied M^rs Willis, there is *none*. Every house in this village, from the sweetness of the Situation, & the purity of the Air, in which neither Misery, Illhealth, or Vice are ever wafted, is inhabited. And yet, (after a short pause) there is a Family, who tho' warmly attached to the spot, yet from a peculiar Generosity of Disposition would perhaps be willing to oblige you with[1] their house." He eagerly caught at this idea, and having gained a direction to the place,[2] he set off immediately on his walk to it. As he approached the House, he was delighted with its situation. It was in the exact centre

[1] the remainder of *erased*.
[2] House *erased*.

of

of a small circular paddock, which was
enclosed by a regular paling, & bordered
with a plantation of Lombardy poplars, &
Spruce firs alternatively placed in three
rows. A gravel walk ran through this
beautiful Shrubbery, and as the remainder
of the paddock was unincumbered with any
other Timber, the surface of it perfectly
even & smooth, and grazed by four white
Cows which were disposed at equal distances
from each other, the whole appearance of
the place as M^r Gower entered the Paddock
was uncommonly striking. A beautifully-
rounded, gravel road without any turn or
interruption led immediately to the house.
M^r Gower rang—the Door was soon opened.
"Are M^r & M^rs Webb at home?" "My
Good Sir they are"—replied the Servant;
And leading the way, conducted M^r Gower
upstairs into a very elegant Dressing room,
where a Lady rising from her seat, welcomed
him with all the Generosity which M^rs Willis
had attributed to the Family.

"Welcome best of Men—Welcome to this
House

House, & to everything it contains. William,
tell your Master of the happiness I enjoy—
invite him to partake of it—. Bring up some
Chocolate immediately; Spread a Cloth in
the dining Parlour, and carry in the venison
pasty—. In the mean time let the Gentleman have some sandwiches, and bring in a
Basket of Fruit—Send up some Ices and
a bason of Soup, and do not forget some
Jellies and Cakes." Then turning to M^r
Gower, & taking out her purse, "Accept
this my good Sir,—. Beleive me you are
welcome to everything that is in my power
to bestow.— I wish my purse were weightier,
but M^r Webb must make up my defi-
ciences—. I know he has cash in the house
to the amount of an hundred pounds, which
he shall bring you immediately." M^r Gower
felt overpowered by her generosity as he put
the purse in his pocket, and from the excess[1]
of his Gratitude, could scarcely express
himself intelligibly when he accepted her
offer of the hundred pounds. M^r Webb

[1] effusions *erased*.

soon

soon entered the room, and repeated every
protestation of Freindship & Cordiality
which his Lady had already made.[1] The
Chocolate, The Sandwiches, the Jellies, the
Cakes, the Ice, and the Soup soon made
their appearance, and M^r Gower having
tasted something of all, and pocketted the
rest, was conducted into the dining parlour,
where he eat a most excellent Dinner & par-
took of the most exquisite Wines, while
M^r and M^rs Webb stood by him still pressing
him to eat and drink a little more. "And
now my good Sir, said M^r Webb, when
M^r Gower's repast was concluded, what else
can we do to contribute to your happiness
and express the Affection we bear you.[2]
Tell us what you wish more to receive, and
depend upon our gratitude for the communication of your wishes." "Give me
then your house & Grounds; I ask for
nothing else." "It is yours, exclaimed both
at once; from this moment it is yours."

---

[1] before expressed *erased*.
[2] for *erased before* you.

This

This Agreement concluded on and the present accepted by M^r Gower, M^r Webb rang to have the Carriage ordered, telling William at the same time to call the Young Ladies.

"Best of Men, said M^rs Webb, we will not long intrude upon your Time."

"Make no Apologies dear Madam, replied M^r Gower, You are welcome to stay this half hour if you like it."

They both burst forth into raptures of Admiration at his politeness, which they agreed served only to make their Conduct appear more inexcusable in trespassing on his time.

The Young Ladies soon entered the room. The eldest of them was about seventeen, the other, several years younger. M^r Gower had no sooner fixed his Eyes on Miss Webb than he felt that something more was necessary to his happiness than the house he had just received—M^rs Webb introduced him to her daughter. "Our dear freind M^r Gower my Love—He has been so good as to accept of this house, small as it is, & to promise to

keep

keep it for ever." "Give me leave to assure
you Sir, said Miss Webb, that I am highly
sensible of your kindness in this respect,
which from the shortness of my Father's &
Mother's acquaintance with you, is more
than usually flattering."

M^r Gower bowed—"You are too obliging
Ma'am—I assure you that I like the house
extremely—and if they would complete
their generosity by giving me their elder
daughter in marriage with a handsome por-
tion, I should have nothing more to wish
for." This compliment brought a blush into
the cheeks of the lovely Miss Webb, who
seemed however to refer herself to her father
& Mother. *They* looked delighted at each
other—At length M^rs Webb breaking silence,
said—"We bend under a weight of obligations to you which we can never repay.
Take our girl, take our Maria, and on her
must the difficult task fall, of endeavouring
to make some return to so much Bene-
fiscence." M^r Webb added, "Her fortune is
but ten thousand pounds, which is almost
too

too small a sum to be offered." This objection however being instantly removed by
the generosity of M^r Gower, who declared
himself satisfied with the sum mentioned,
M^r & M^rs Webb, with their youngest daughter
took their leave, and on the next day, the
nuptials of their eldest with M^r Gower were
celebrated.—This amiable Man now found
himself perfectly happy; united to a very
lovely and deserving young woman, with an
handsome fortune, an elegant house, settled
in the village of Evelyn, & by that means
enabled to cultivate his acquaintance with
M^rs Willis, could he have a wish ungratified?
—For some months he found that he could
*not*, till one day as he was walking in the
Shrubbery with Maria leaning on his arm,
they observed a rose full-blown lying on the
gravel; it had fallen from a rose tree which
with three others had been planted by
M^r Webb to give a pleasing variety to the
walk. These four Rose trees served also to
mark the quarters of the Shrubbery, by
which means the Traveller might always
know

know how far in his progress round the
Paddock he was got—. Maria stooped to
pick up the beautiful flower, and with all
her Family Generosity presented it to her
Husband. "My dear Frederic, said she, pray
take this charming rose." "Rose! exclaimed
M^r Gower—. Oh! Maria, of what does not
that remind me! Alas my poor Sister, how
have I neglected you!" The truth was that
M^r Gower was the only son of a very large
Family, of which Miss Rose Gower was the
thirteenth daughter. This Young Lady
whose merits deserved a better fate than
she met with, was the darling of her relations—From the clearness of her skin & the
Brilliancy of her Eyes, she was fully entitled
to all their partial affection. Another circumstance contributed to the general Love
they bore her, and that was one of the finest
heads of hair in the world. A few Months
before her Brother's marriage, her heart
had been engaged by the attentions and
charms of a young Man whose high rank and
expectations seemed to foretell objections
from

from his Family to a match which would be highly desirable to theirs. Proposals were made on the young Man's part, and proper objections on his Father's—He was desired to return from Carlisle where he was with his beloved Rose, to the family seat in Sussex. He was obliged to comply, and the angry father then finding from his Conversation how determined he was to marry no other woman, sent him for a fortnight to the Isle of Wight under the care of the Family Chaplain, with the hope of overcoming his Constancy by Time and Absence in a foreign Country. They accordingly prepared to bid a long adeiu to England— The young Nobleman was not allowed to see his Rosa. They set sail—A storm arose which baffled the arts of the Seamen. The Vessel was wrecked on the coast of Calshot and every Soul on board perished. This sad Event soon reached Carlisle, and the beautiful Rose was affected by it, beyond the power of Expression. It was to soften her affliction by obtaining a picture of her unfortunate

fortunate Lover that her brother undertook
a Journey into Sussex, where he hoped that
his petition would not be rejected, by the
severe yet afflicted Father. When he reached
Evelyn he was not many miles from ——
Castle, but the pleasing events which befell
him in that place had for a while made him
totally forget the object of his Journey &
his unhappy Sister. The little incident of the
rose however brought everything concerning
her to his recollection again, & he bitterly
repented his neglect. He returned to the
house immediately and agitated by[1] Greif,
Apprehension and Shame wrote the following Letter to Rosa.

July 14<sup>th</sup>—. Evelyn

MY DEAREST SISTER

As it is now four months since I left
Carlisle, during which period I have not
once written to you, You will perhaps un-
justly accuse me of Neglect and Forget-
fulness. Alas! I blush when I own the truth
of your Accusation.—Yet if you are still

¹ with *erased*.

alive,

alive, do not think too harshly of me, or suppose that I could for a moment forget the situation of my Rose. Beleive me I will forget you no longer, but will hasten as soon as possible to —— Castle if I find by your answer that you are still alive. Maria joins me in every dutiful and affectionate wish, & I am yours sincerely

F. GOWER.

He waited in the most anxious expectation for an answer to his Letter, which arrived as soon as the great distance from Carlisle would admit of.—But alas, it came not from[1] Rosa.

Carlisle July 17th

DEAR BROTHER

My Mother has taken the liberty of opening your Letter to poor Rose, as she has been dead these six weeks. Your long absence and continued Silence gave us all great uneasiness and hastened her to the Grave. Your Journey to —— Castle therefore may be spared. You do not tell us

[1] for *erased.*

where you have been since the time of your quitting Carlisle, nor in any way account for your tedious absence, which gives us some surprise. We all unite in Comp^{ts} to Maria, & beg to know who she is—.

Y^r affec:^{te} Sister<br>M. GOWER.

This Letter, by which M^r Gower was obliged to attribute to his own conduct, his Sister's death, was so violent a shock to his feelings, that in spite of his living at Evelyn where Illness was scarcely ever heard of, he was attacked by a fit of the gout, which confining him to his own room afforded an opportunity to Maria of shining in that favourite character of Sir Charles Grandison's, a nurse. No woman could ever appear more amiable than Maria did under such circumstances, and at last by her unremitting attentions had the pleasure of seeing him gradually recover the use of his feet. It was a blessing by no means lost on him, for he was no sooner in a condition to

leave

leave the house, than he mounted his horse,
and rode to —— Castle, wishing to find
whether his Lordship softened by his Son's
death, might have been brought to consent
to the match, had both he and Rosa been
alive. His amiable Maria followed him with
her Eyes till she could see him no longer,
and then sinking into her chair overwhelmed
with Greif, found that in his absence she
could enjoy no comfort.

Mr Gower arrived late in the evening at
the castle, which was situated on a woody
Eminence commanding a beautiful prospect
of the Sea. Mr Gower did not dislike the
situation, tho' it was certainly greatly
inferior[1] to that of his own house. There was
an irregularity in the fall of the ground, and
a profusion of old Timber which appeared
to him illsuited to the stile of the Castle, for
it being a building of a very ancient[2] date,
he thought it required the Paddock of
Evelyn lodge to form a Contrast, and enliven
the structure. The gloomy appearance of

[1] superior *erased*.                [2] old *erased*.

the

the old Castle frowning on him as he followed
it's winding approach, struck him with
terror. Nor did he think himself safe, till
he was introduced into the Drawing room
where the Family were assembled to tea.
M^r Gower was a perfect stranger to every
one in the Circle but tho' he was always
timid in the Dark and easily terrified when
alone, he did not want that more necessary
and more noble courage which enabled him
without a Blush to enter a large party of
superior Rank, whom he had never seen
before, & to take his Seat amongst them
with perfect Indifference. The name of
Gower was not unknown to Lord ——. He
felt distressed & astonished; yet rose and
received him with all the politeness of a
well-bred Man. Lady —— who felt a deeper
sorrow at the loss of her Son, than his
Lordships harder heart was capable of,
could hardly keep her Seat when she found
that he was the Brother of her lamented
Henry's[1] Rosa. "My Lord said M^r Gower

[1] *Erasure illegible.*

as

as soon as he was seated, You are perhaps surprised at receiving a visit from a Man whom you could not have the least expectation of seeing here. But my Sister my unfortunate Sister is the real cause of my thus troubling you: That luckless Girl is now no more—and tho' *she* can receive no pleasure from the intelligence, yet for the satisfaction of her Family I wish to know whether the Death of this unhappy Pair has made an impression on your heart sufficiently strong to obtain that consent to their Marriage which in happier circumstances you would not be persuaded to give supposing that they now were both alive." His Lordship seemed lossed in astonishment. Lady —— could not support the mention of her son, and left the room in tears; the rest of the Family remained attentively listening, almost persuaded that M^r Gower was distracted. "M^r Gower, replied his Lordship This is a very odd question—It appears to me that you are supposing an impossibility—No one can more sincerely regret

regret the death of my Son than I have always done, and it gives me great concern to know that Miss Gower's was hastened by his—. Yet to suppose them alive is destroying at once the Motive for a change in my sentiments concerning the affair." "My Lord, replied M^r Gower in anger, I see that you are a most inflexible Man, and that not even the death of your Son can make you wish his future Life happy. I will no longer detain your Lordship. I see, I plainly see that you are a very vile Man—And now I have the honour of wishing all your Lordships, and Ladyships a good Night." He immediately left the room, forgetting in the heat of his Anger the lateness of the hour, which at any other time would have made him tremble, & leaving the whole Company unanimous in their opinion of his being Mad. When however he had mounted his horse and the great Gates of the Castle had shut him out, he felt an universal tremor through out his whole frame. If we consider his Situation indeed, alone, on horseback, as late

late in the year as August, and in the day,
as nine o'clock, with no light to direct him
but that of the Moon almost full, and the
Stars which alarmed him by their twinkling,
who can refrain from pitying him?—No
house within a quarter of a mile, and a
Gloomy Castle blackened by the deep shade
of Walnuts and Pines, behind him.—He felt
indeed almost distracted with his fears, and
shutting his Eyes till he arrived at the
Village to prevent his seeing either Gipsies
or Ghosts, he rode on a full gallop all the
way. On his return home, he rang the house-
bell, but no one appeared, a second time he
rang, but the door was not opened, a third
& a fourth with as little success, when observing the dining parlour window open he
leapt in, & persued his way through the
house till he reached Maria's Dressingroom,
where he found all the servants assembled
at tea. Surprized at so very unusual a sight,
he fainted, on his recovery he found himself
on the Sofa, with his wife's maid kneeling
by him, chafing his temples with Hungary
water

water—. From her he learned that his beloved Maria had been so much grieved at
his departure that she died of a broken
heart about 3 hours after his departure.

He then became sufficiently composed to
give necessary orders for her funeral which
took place the Monday following this being
the Saturday—When M^r Gower had settled
the order of the procession he set out himself
to Carlisle, to give vent to his sorrow in the
bosom of his family—He arrived there in
high health & spirits, after a delightful
journey of 3 days & a ½—What was his
surprize on entering the Breakfast parlour
to see Rosa his beloved Rosa seated on a
Sofa; at the sight of him she fainted &
would have fallen had not a Gentleman
sitting with his back to the door, started up
& saved her from sinking to the ground—
She very soon came to herself & then introduced this gentleman to her Brother as her
Husband a M^r Davenport—

But my dearest Rosa said the astonished
Gower, I thought you were dead & buried.

Why

Why my dr Frederick replied Rosa I wished
you to think so, hoping that you would
spread the report about the country & it
would thus by some means reach —— Castle
—By this I hoped some how or other to touch
the hearts of its inhabitants. It was not till
the day before yesterday that I heard of the
death of my beloved Henry which I learned
from Mr D—— who concluded by offering
me his hand. I accepted it with transport,
& was married yesterday—Mr Gower, em-
braced his sister & shook hands with Mr
Davenport, he then took a stroll into the town
—As he passed by a public house he called
for a pot of beer, which was brought him
immediately by his old friend Mrs Willis—

Great was his astonishment at seeing Mrs
Willis in Carlisle. But not forgetful of the
respect he owed her, he dropped on one knee,
& received the frothy cup from her, more
grateful to him than Nectar—He instantly
made her an offer of his hand & heart, which
she graciously condescended to accept, telling him that she was only on a visit to her
cousin

cousin, who kept the *Anchor* & should be
ready to return to Evelyn, whenever he
chose—The next morning they were married
& immediately proceeded to Evelyn—When
he reached home, he recollected that he had
never written to M^r & M^rs Webb to inform
them of the death of their daughter, which
he rightly supposed they knew nothing of, as
they never took in any newspapers—He immediately dispatched the following Letter—

Evelyn—Aug^st 19^th 1809—
DEAREST MADAM,

How can words express the poignancy
of my feelings! Our Maria, our beloved
Maria is no more, she breathed her last, on
Saturday the 12^th of Aug^st—I see you now
in an agony of grief lamenting not your own,
but my loss—Rest satisfied I am happy,
possessed of my lovely Sarah what more
can I wish for?—

I remain
respectfully Yours
F. GOWER
Westgate

Westgate Buil^gs Aug^st 22^d

GENEROUS, BEST OF MEN

how truly we rejoice to hear of your
present welfare & happiness! & how truly
grateful are we for your unexampled generosity in writing to condole with us on the late
unlucky accident which befel our Maria—
I have enclosed a draught on our banker
for 30 pounds, which M^r Webb joins with
me in entreating you & the aimiable Sarah
to accept—

Your most grateful

ANNE AUGUSTA WEBB


M^r & M^rs Gower resided many years at
Evelyn enjoying perfect happiness the just
reward of their virtues. The only alteration
which took place at Evelyn was that M^r &
M^rs Davenport settled there in M^rs Willis's
former abode & were for many years the
proprietors of the White horse Inn—



CATHARINE

# CATHARINE

## OR THE BOWER

*To*

## To Miss Austen

MADAM

Encouraged by your warm patronage of The beautiful Cassandra, and The History of England, which through your generous support, have obtained a place in every library in the Kingdom, and run through threescore Editions, I take the liberty of begging the same Exertions in favour of the following Novel, which I humbly flatter myself, possesses Merit beyond any already published, or any that will ever in future appear, except such as may proceed from the pen of Your Most Grateful Humble Serv<sup>t</sup>

THE AUTHOR

Steventon August 1792—

**CATHARINE**

# CATHARINE[1]

## OR THE BOWER

———

CATHARINE[1] had the misfortune, as many heroines have had before her, of losing her Parents when she was very young, and of being brought up under the care of a Maiden Aunt, who while she tenderly loved her, watched over her conduct with so scrutinizing a severity, as to make it very doubtful to many people, and to Catharine[1] amongst the rest, whether she loved her or not. She had frequently been deprived of a real pleasure through this jealous Caution, had been sometimes obliged to relinquish a Ball because an Officer was to be there, or to dance with a Partner of her Aunt's introduction in preference to one of her own Choice. But her Spirits were naturally good, and not easily depressed, and she

[1] Kitty, *erased here, stands elsewhere.*

possessed

possessed such a fund of vivacity and good humour as could only be damped by some very serious vexation.—Besides these antidotes against every disappointment, and consolations under them, she had another, which afforded her constant releif in all her misfortunes, and that was a fine shady Bower, the work of her own infantine Labours assisted by those of two young Companions who had resided in the same village—. To this Bower,[1] which terminated a very pleasant and retired walk in her Aunt's Garden, she always wandered whenever anything disturbed her, and it possessed such a charm over her senses, as constantly to tranquillize her mind & quiet her spirits— Solitude & reflection might perhaps have had the same effect in her Bed Chamber, yet Habit had so strengthened the idea which Fancy had first suggested, that such a thought never occurred to Kitty who was firmly persuaded that her Bower alone could restore her to herself. Her imagination was

[1] Garden *erased*.

warm

warm, and in her Freindships, as well as in
the whole tenure of her Mind, she was
enthousiastic. This beloved Bower had been
the united work of herself and two amiable
Girls, for whom since her earliest Years, she
had felt the tenderest regard. They were
the daughters of the Clergyman of the
Parish with whose Family, while it had continued there, her Aunt had been on the most
intimate terms, and the little Girls tho'
separated for the greatest part of the Year
by the different Modes of their Education,
were constantly together during the holidays
of the Miss Wynnes; [they were companions
in their walks, their Schemes & Amusements,
and while the sweetness of their dispositions
had prevented any serious Quarrels, the
trifling disputes which it was impossible
wholly to avoid, had been far from lessening
their affection].[1] In those days of happy
Childhood, now so often regretted by Kitty
this arbour had been formed, and separated
perhaps for ever from these dear freinds, it

[1] *Erased.*

D encouraged

encouraged more than any other place the
tender and Melancholly recollections of
hours rendered pleasant by *them*, at one [*sic*]
so sorrowful, yet so soothing! It was now two
years since the death of M^r Wynne, and the
consequent dispersion of his Family who
had been left by it in great distress. They
had been reduced to a state of absolute
dependance on some relations, who though
very opulent, and very nearly connected
with them, had with difficulty been prevailed
on to contribute anything towards their
Support. M^rs Wynne was fortunately spared
the knowledge & participation of their
distress, by her release from a painful illness
a few months before the death of her husband.—The eldest daughter had been obliged
to accept the offer of one of her cousins to
equip her for the East Indies, and tho'
infinitely against her inclinations had been
necessitated to embrace the only possibility
that was offered to her, of a Maintenance;
Yet it was *one*, so opposite to all her ideas
of Propriety, so contrary to her Wishes,

so

so repugnant to her feelings, that she would almost have preferred Servitude to it, had Choice been allowed her—. Her personal Attractions had gained her a husband as soon as she had arrived at Bengal, and she had now been married nearly a twelve-month. Splendidly, yet unhappily married. United to a Man of double her own age, whose disposition was not amiable, and whose Manners were unpleasing, though his Character was respectable. Kitty had heard twice from her freind since her marriage, but her Letters were always unsatisfactory, and though she did not openly avow her feelings, yet every line proved her to be Unhappy. She spoke with pleasure of nothing, but of those Amusements which they had shared together and which could return no more, and seemed to have no happiness in veiw but that of returning to England again. Her sister had been taken by another relation the Dowager Lady Halifax as a companion to her Daughters, and had accompanied her family into Scot-land

land about the same time of Cecilia's leaving
England. From Mary therefore Kitty had the
power of hearing more frequently, but her
Letters were scarcely more comfortable—.
There was not indeed that hopelessness of
sorrow in her situation as in her sisters; she
was not married, and could yet look forward
to a change in her circumstances, but
situated for the present without any immediate hope of it, in a family where, tho' all
were her relations she had no freind, she
wrote usually in depressed Spirits, which her
separation from her Sister and her Sister's
Marriage had greatly contributed to make
so.—Divided thus from the two she loved
best on Earth, while Cecilia & Mary were
still more endeared to her by their loss,
everything that brought a remembrance of
them was doubly cherished, & the Shrubs
they had planted, & the keepsakes they had
given were rendered sacred—. The living
of Chetwynde was now in the possession
of a M<sup>r</sup> Dudley, whose Family unlike the
Wynnes were productive only of vexation &
                                        trouble

trouble to M^rs Percival[1] and her Neice.
M^r Dudley, who was the Younger Son of a
very noble Family, of a Family more famed
for their Pride than their opulence, tenacious
of his Dignity, and jealous of his rights,
was forever quarrelling, if not with M^rs P.
herself, with her Steward and Tenants
concerning tythes, and with the principal
Neighbours themselves concerning the respect & parade, he exacted. His Wife, an
ill-educated, untaught woman of ancient
family, was proud of that family almost
without knowing why, and like him too
was haughty and quarrelsome, without considering for what. Their only daughter,
who inherited the ignorance, the insolence,
& pride of her parents, was from that Beauty
of which she was unreasonably vain, considered by them as an irresistable Creature,
and looked up to as the future restorer, by
a Splendid Marriage, of the dignity which
their reduced Situation and M^r Dudley's
being obliged to take orders for a Country

[1] *Substituted here and elsewhere for* Peterson.

Living

Living had so much lessened. They at once
despised the Percivals as people of mean[1]
family, and envied them as people of fortune. They were jealous of their being more
respected than themselves and while they
affected to consider them as of no Consequence, were continually seeking to lessen
them in the opinion of the Neighbourhood
by Scandalous & Malicious reports. Such a
family as this, was ill-calculated to console
Kitty for the loss of the Wynnes, or to fill
up by their Society, those occasionally irk-
some hours which in so retired a Situation
would sometimes occur for want of a Companion. Her aunt was most excessively
fond of her, and miserable if she saw her for
a moment out of spirits; Yet she lived in
such constant apprehension of her marrying
imprudently if she were allowed the opportunity of choosing, and was so dissatisfied
with her behaviour when she saw her with
Young Men, for it was, from her natural
disposition remarkably open and un-

---

[1] no *erased*.

reserved

reserved, that though she frequently wished
for her Neice's sake, that the Neighbourhood
were larger, and that She had used herself
to mix more with it, yet the recollection of
there being young Men in almost every
Family in it, always conquered the Wish.
The same fears that prevented M^{rs} Peterson's joining much in the Society of her
Neighbours, led her equally to avoid inviting her relations to spend any time in her
House—She had therefore constantly regretted the annual attempt of a distant
relation to visit her at Chetwynde, as there
was a young Man in the Family of whom
she had heard many traits that alarmed her.
This Son was however now on his travels,
and the repeated solicitations of Kitty,
joined to a consciousness of having declined
with too little Ceremony the frequent over-
tures[1] of her Freinds to be admitted, and a
real wish to see them herself, easily prevailed on her to press with great Earnestness
the pleasure of a visit from them during the

[1] *Erasure illegible.*

Summer

Summer. M^r & M^rs Stanley were accordingly
to come, and Catharine, in having an object
to look forward to, a something to expect
that must inevitably releive the dullness of
a constant tete a tete with her Aunt, was
so delighted, and her spirits so elevated,
that for the three or four days immediately
preceding their Arrival, she could scarcely
fix herself to any employment. In this point
M^rs Percival always thought her defective,
and frequently complained of a want of
Steadiness & perseverance in her occupations, which were by no means congenial to
the eagerness of Kitty's Disposition, and
perhaps not often met with in any young
person. The tediousness too of her Aunt's
conversation ˅ and the want of agreable
Companions greatly increased this desire of
Change in her Employments, for Kitty
found herself much sooner tired of Reading,
Working, or Drawing, in M^rs Peterson's
parlour than in her own Arbour, where
M^rs Peterson for fear of its being damp never
accompanied her.

As

As her Aunt prided herself on the exact propriety and Neatness with which every-thing in her Family was conducted, and had no higher Satisfaction than that of knowing her house to be always in complete Order, as her fortune was good, and her Establishment Ample, few were the preparations necessary for the reception of her Visitors. The day of their arrival so long expected, at length came,[1] and the Noise of the Coach & 4 as it drove round the sweep, was to Catherine a more interesting sound, than the Music of an Italian Opera, which to most Heroines is the hight of Enjoyment. M^r and M^rs Stanley were people of Large Fortune & high Fashion. He was a Member of the house of Commons, and they were therefore most agreably necessitated to reside half the Year in Town; where Miss Stanley had been attended by the most capital Masters from the time of her being six years old to the last Spring, which comprehending a period of twelve Years had been dedicated

[1] arrived *erased.*

to

to the acquirement of Accomplishments
which were now to be displayed and in a few
Years entirely neglected. She was[1] not inelegant in her appearance, rather handsome,
and naturally not deficient in Abilities; but
those Years which ought to have been spent
in the attainment of useful knowledge and
Mental Improvement, had been all bestowed
in learning Drawing, Italian and Music,
more especially the latter, and she now
united to these Accomplishments, an Understanding unimproved by reading and a
Mind totally devoid either of Taste or
Judgement. Her temper was by Nature
good, but unassisted by reflection, she had
neither patience under Disappointment, nor
could sacrifice her own inclinations to pro-
mote the happiness of others. All her Ideas
were towards the Elegance of her appearance, the fashion of her dress, and the
Admiration she wished them to excite. She
professed a love of Books without Reading,
was Lively without Wit, and generally

[1] about Kitty's age *erased*.

good

good humoured without Merit. Such was
Camilla Stanley; and Catherine, who was
prejudiced by her appearance, and who
from her solitary Situation was ready to
like anyone, tho' her Understanding and
Judgement would not otherwise have been
easily satisfied, felt almost convinced when
she saw her, that Miss Stanley would be the
very companion She wanted, and in some
degree make amends for the loss of Cecilia
& Mary Wynne. She therefore attached herself to Camilla from the first day of her
arrival, and from being the only young
People in the house, they were by inclina-
tion constant Companions. Kitty was herself a great reader, tho' perhaps not a very
deep one, and felt therefore highly delighted
to find that Miss Stanley was equally fond
of it. Eager to know that their sentiments
as to Books were similar, she very soon
began questioning her new Acquaintance
on the subject; but though She was well
read in Modern history herself, she chose
rather to speak first of Books of a lighter
kind

kind, of Books universally read and Admired. [and that have given rise perhaps to more frequent Arguments than any other of the same sort].[1]

"You have read M^rs Smith's Novels, I suppose?" said she to her Companion—. "Oh! Yes, replied the other, and I am quite delighted with them—They are the sweetest things in the world—" "And which do you prefer of them?" "Oh! dear, I think there is no comparison between them—Emmeline is *so much* better than any of the others—" "Many people think so, I know; but there does not appear so great a disproportion in their Merits to *me*; do you think it is better written?" "Oh! I do not know anything about *that*—but it is better in *everything*— Besides, Ethelinde is so long—" "That is a very common Objection I believe, said Kitty, but for my own part, if a book is well written, I always find it too short." "So do I, only I get tired of it before it is finished." "But did not you find the story of Ethelinde

------

[1] *Erased.*

very

very interesting? And the Descriptions of
Grasmere, are not the⟨y⟩ Beautiful?" "Oh!
I missed them all, because I was in such a
hurry to know the end of it—Then from an
easy transition she added, We are going to
the Lakes this Autumn, and I am quite
Mad with Joy; Sir Henry Devereux has
promised to go with us, and that will make
it so pleasant, you know—"

"I dare say it will; but I think it is a pity
that Sir Henry's powers of pleasing were not
reserved for an occasion where they might
be more wanted.—However I quite envy
you the pleasure of such a Scheme." "Oh!
I am quite delighted with the thoughts of
it; I can think of nothing else. I assure you
I have done nothing for this last Month but
plan what Cloathes I should take with me,
and I have at last determined to take very
few indeed besides my travelling Dress, and
so I advise you to do, when ever you go;
for I intend in case we should fall in with
any races, or stop at Matlock or Scarborough,
to have some Things made for the occasion."

You

"You intend then to go into Yorkshire?"

"I beleive not—indeed I know nothing of the Route, for I never trouble myself about such things—. I only know that we are to go from Derbyshire to Matlock and Scarborough, but to which of them first, I neither know nor care—I am in hopes of meeting some particular freinds of mine at Scarborough—Augusta told me in her last Letter that Sir Peter talked of going; but then you know that is so uncertain. I cannot bear Sir Peter, he is such a horrid Creature—"

"He *is*, is he?" said Kitty, not knowing what else to say. "Oh! he is quite Shocking." Here the Conversation was interrupted, and Kitty was left in a painful Uncertainty, as to the particulars of Sir Peter's Character; She knew only that he was Horrid and Shocking, but why, and in what, yet remained to be discovered. She could scarcely resolve what to think of her new Acquaintance; She appeared to be shamefully ignorant as to the Geography of England,

if

if she had understood her right, and equally devoid of Taste and Information. Kitty was however unwilling to decide hastily; she was at once desirous of doing Miss Stanley justice, and of having her own Wishes in her answered; she determined therefore to suspend all Judgement for some time. After Supper, the Conversation turning on the state of Affairs in the political World, M^rs P, who was firmly of opinion that the whole race of Mankind were degenerating, said that for her part, Everything she beleived was going to rack and ruin, all order was destroyed over the face of the World, The house of Commons she heard did not break up sometimes till five in the Morning, and Depravity never was so general before; concluding with a wish that she might live to see the Manners of the People in Queen Elizabeth's reign, restored again. "Well Ma'am, said her Neice, [I beleive you have as good a chance of it as any one else]¹ but I hope you do not mean

¹ *Erased.*

with

with the times to restore Queen Eliz^th
herself."

"Queen Eliz^th, said M^rs Stanley who
never hazarded a remark on History that
was not well founded, lived to a good old
age, and was a very Clever Woman."
"True Ma'am, said Kitty; but I do not
consider either of those Circumstances as
meritorious in herself, and they are very far
from making me wish her return, for if she
were to come again with the same Abilities
and the same good Constitution She might
do as much Mischief and last as long as she
did before—then turning to Camilla who
had been sitting very silent for some time, she
added, What do *you* think of Elizabeth Miss
Stanley? I hope you will not defend her."

"Oh! dear, said Miss Stanley, I know
nothing of Politics, and cannot bear to hear
them mentioned." Kitty started at this
repulse, but made no answer; that Miss
Stanley must be ignorant of what she could
not distinguish from Politics[1] she felt per-

[1] History *erased.*

fectly

fectly convinced.—She retired to her own
room, perplexed in her opinion about her
new Acquaintance, and fearful of her being
very unlike Cecilia and Mary. She arose the
next morning to experience a fuller conviction of this, and every future day en-
creased it—. She found no variety in her
conversation; She received no information
from her but in fashions, and no Amusement
but in her performance on the Harpsichord;
and after repeated endeavours to find her
what she wished, she was obliged to give up
the attempt and to consider it as fruitless.
There had occasionally appeared a something like humour in Camilla which had
inspired her with hopes, that she might at
least have a natural genius, tho' not an
improved one, but these Sparklings of Wit
happened so seldom, and were so ill-sup-
ported that she was at last convinced of
their being merely accidental. All her stock
of knowledge was exhausted in a very few
Days, and when Kitty had learnt from her,
how large their house in Town was, when

the fashionable Amusements began, who
were the celebrated Beauties and who the
best Millener, Camilla had nothing further
to teach, except the Characters of any of her
Acquaintance as they occurred in Conversation, which was done with equal Ease
and Brevity, by saying that the person was
either the sweetest Creature in the world,
and one of whom she was doatingly fond,
or horrid, shocking and not fit to be seen.

As Catherine was very desirous of gaining
every possible information as to the Characters of the Halifax Family, and concluded
that Miss Stanley must be acquainted with
them, as she seemed to be so with every one
of any Consequence, she took an opportunity
as Camilla was one day enumerating all the
people of rank that her Mother visited, of
asking her whether Lady Halifax were
among the number.

"Oh! Thank you for reminding me of her,
She is the sweetest Woman in the world,
and one of our most intimate Acquaintances,
I do not suppose there is a day passes during
the

the six Months that we are in Town, but
what we see each other in the course of it—.
And I correspond with all the Girls."

"They *are* then a very pleasant Family?
said Kitty. They ought to be so indeed, to
allow of such frequent Meetings, or all
Conversation must be at end."

"Oh! dear, not at all, said Miss Stanley,
for sometimes we do not speak to each other
for a month together. We meet perhaps only
in Public, and then you know we are often
not[1] able to get near enough; but in that
case we always nod & smile."

"Which does just as well—. But I was
going to ask you whether you have ever
seen a Miss Wynne with them?"

"I know who you mean perfectly—she
wears a blue hat—. I have frequently seen
her in Brook Street, when I have been at
Lady Halifax's Balls—She gives one every
Month during the Winter—. But only
think how good it is in her to take care of
Miss Wynne, for she is a very distant rela-

[1] not always *erased*.

tion

tion, and so poor that, as Miss Halifax told me, her Mother was obliged to find her in Cloathes. Is not it shameful?"

"That she should be so poor? it is indeed, with such wealthy connexions as the Family have."

"Oh! no; I mean, was not it shameful in M^r Wynne to leave his Children so distressed, when he had actually the Living of Chetwynde and two or three Curacies, and only four Children to provide for—. What would he have done if he had had ten, as many people have?"

"He would have given them all a good Education and have left them all equally poor."

"Well I do think there never was so lucky a Family. Sir George Fitzgibbon you know sent the eldest girl to India entirely at his own Expence, where they say she is most nobly married and the happiest Creature in the World—Lady Halifax you see has taken care of the youngest and treats her as if she were her Daughter; She does

does not go out into Public with her to be
sure; but then she is always present when
her Ladyship gives her Balls, and nothing
can be kinder to her than Lady Halifax is;
she would have taken her to Cheltenham
last year, if there had been room enough at
the Lodgings, and therefore I dont think
that *she* can have anything to complain of.
Then there are the two Sons; one of them the
Bishop of M—— has got into the Army[1] as
a Leiutenant I suppose; and the other is
extremely well off I know, for I have a notion
that somebody puts him to School some-
where in Wales. Perhaps you knew them
when they lived here?"

"Very well,[2] We met as often as your
Family and the Halifaxes do in Town, but
as we seldom had any difficulty in getting
near enough to speak, we seldom parted
with merely a Nod & a Smile. They were
indeed a most charming Family, and I
beleive have scarcely their Equals in the
World; The Neighbours we now have at

---

[1] sent to Sea *erased*.          [2] Slightly *erased*.

the

the Parsonage, appear to more disadvantage in coming after them."

"Oh! horrid Wretches! I wonder you can endure them."

"Why, what would you have one do?"

"Oh! Lord, If I were in your place, I should abuse them all day long."

"So I do, but it does no good."

"Well, I declare it is quite a pity that they should be suffered to live. I wish my Father would propose knocking all their Brains out, some day or other when he is in the House. So abominably proud of their Family! And I dare say after all, that there is nothing particular in it."

"Why Yes, I beleive they *have* reason to value themselves on it, if any body has; for you know he is Lord Amyatt's Brother."

"Oh! I know all that very well, but it is no reason for their being so horrid. I remember I met Miss Dudley last Spring with Lady Amyatt at Ranelagh, and she had such a frightful Cap on, that I have never been able to bear any of them since.—And so you
used

used to think the Wynnes very pleasant?"
"You speak as if their being so were doubtful! Pleasant! Oh! they were every thing
that could interest and attach. It is not in
my power to do Justice to their Merits,
tho' not to feel them, I think must be
impossible. They have unfitted me for any
Society but their own!"

"Well, That is just what I think of the
Miss Halifaxes; by the bye, I must write to
Caroline tomorrow, and I do not know what
to say to her. The Barlows[1] too are just
such other sweet Girls; but I wish Augusta's
hair was not so dark. I cannot bear Sir
Peter—Horrid Wretch! He is *always* laid
up with the Gout, which is exceedingly disagreable to the Family."

"And perhaps not very pleasant to *himself*—. But as to the Wynnes; do you really
think them very fortunate?"

"Do I? Why, does not every body? Miss
Halifax & Caroline & Maria all say that they
are the luckiest Creatures in the World.

[1] Barkers *erased*.

So

So does Sir George Fitzgibbon and so do
Every body."

"That is, Every body who have themselves conferred an obligation on them. But
do you call it lucky, for a Girl of Genius &
Feeling to be sent in quest of a Husband to
Bengal, to be married there to a Man of
whose Disposition she has no opportunity of
judging till her Judgement is of no use to
her, who may be a Tyrant, or a Fool or both
for what she knows to the Contrary. Do
you call *that* fortunate?"

"I know nothing of all that; I only know
that it was extremely good in Sir George to
fit her out and pay her Passage, and that
she would not have found Many who would
have done the same."

"I wish she had not found *one*, said Kitty
with great Eagerness, she might then have
remained in England and been happy."

"Well, I cannot conceive the hardship of
going out in a very agreable Manner with
two or three sweet Girls for Companions,
having a delightful voyage to Bengal or
Barbadoes

Barbadoes or wherever it is, and being married soon after one's arrival to a very charming Man immensely rich—. I see no hardship in all that."

"Your representation of the Affair, said Kitty laughing, certainly gives a very different idea of it from Mine. But supposing all this to be true, still, as it was by no means certain that she would be so fortunate either in her voyage, her Companions, or her husband; in being obliged to run the risk of their proving very different, she undoubtedly experienced a great hardship—. Besides, to a Girl of any Delicacy, the voyage in itself, since the object of it is so universally known, is a punishment that needs no other to make it very severe."

"I do not see that at all. She is not the first Girl who has gone to the East Indies for a Husband, and I declare I should think it very good fun if I were as poor."

"I beleive you would think very differently *then*. But at least you will not defend her Sister's situation? Dependant even for her

her Cloathes on the bounty of others, who of course do not pity her, as by your own account, they consider her as very fortunate."

"You are extremely nice upon my word; Lady Halifax is a delightful Woman, and one of the sweetest tempered Creatures in the World; I am sure I have every reason to speak well of her, for we are under most amazing Obligations to her. She has frequently chaperoned me when my Mother has been indisposed, and last Spring she lent me her own horse three times, which was a prodigious favour, for it is the most beautiful Creature that ever was seen, and I am the only person she ever lent it to. ["If so, *Mary Wynne* can receive very little advantage from her having it."][1]

And then, continued she, the Miss Halifaxes are quite delightful. Maria is one of the cleverest Girls that ever were known— Draws in Oils, and plays anything by sight. She promised me one of her Drawings before

[1] *Erased.*

I

I left Town, but I entirely forgot to ask her
for it. I would give anything to have one."
[Why indeed, if Maria will give my Freind
a drawing, she can have nothing to complain
of, but as she does not write in Spirits, I
suppose she has not yet been fortunate
enough to be so distinguished.][1] "But was
not it very odd, said Kitty, that the Bishop
should send Charles Wynne to sea, when he
must have had a much better chance of
providing for him in the Church, which was
the profession that Charles liked best, and
the one for which his Father had intended
him? The Bishop I know had often promised Mr Wynne a living, and as he never
gave him one, I think it was incumbant on
him to transfer the promise to his Son."

"I beleive you think he ought to have
resigned his Bishopric to him; you seem
determined to be dissatisfied with every
thing that has been done for them."

"Well, said Kitty, this is a subject on
which we shall never agree, and therefore

[1] *Erased.*

it

it will be useless to continue it farther, or
to mention it again—'' She then left the
room, and running out of the House was
soon in her dear Bower where she could
indulge in peace all her affectionate Anger
against the relations of the Wynnes, which
was greatly heightened by finding from
Camilla that they were in general considered
as having acted particularly well by them—.
She amused herself for some time in Abusing,
and Hating them all, with great spirit, and
when this tribute to her regard for the
Wynnes, was paid, and the Bower began to
have its usual influence over her Spirits, she
contributed towards settling them, by taking
out a book, for she had always one about
her, and reading—. She had been so
employed for nearly an hour, when Camilla
came running towards her with great Eagerness, and apparently great Pleasure—. ''Oh!
my Dear Catherine, said she, half out of
Breath—I have such delightful News for
You—But you shall guess what it is—We
are all the happiest Creatures in the World;
would

would you beleive it, the Dudleys have sent us an invitation to a Ball at their own House—. What Charming People they are! I had no idea of there being so much sense in the whole Family—I declare I quite doat upon them—. And it happens so fortunately too, for I expect a new Cap from Town tomorrow which will just do for a Ball—Gold Net—It will be a most angelic thing—Every Body will be longing for the pattern—" The expectation of a Ball was indeed very agreable intelligence to Kitty, who fond of Dancing and seldom able to enjoy it, had reason to feel even greater pleasure in it than her Freind; for to *her*, it was now no novelty—. Camilla's delight however was by no means inferior to Kitty's, and she rather expressed the most of the two. The Cap came and every other preparation was soon completed; while these were in agitation the Days passed gaily away, but when Directions were no longer necessary, Taste could no longer be displayed, and Difficulties no longer overcome, the short period that

that intervened before the day of the Ball
hung heavily on their hands, and every
hour was too long. The very few Times that
Kitty had ever enjoyed the Amusement of
Dancing was an excuse for *her* impatience,
and an apology for the Idleness it occasioned
to a Mind naturally very Active; but her
Freind without such a plea was infinitely
worse than herself. She could do nothing
but wander from the house to the Garden,
and from the Garden to the avenue, wonder-
ing when Thursday would come, which she
might easily have ascertained, and counting
the hours as they passed which served only
to lengthen them.—. They retired to their
rooms in high Spirits on Wednesday night,
but Kitty awoke the next Morning with a
violent Toothake. It was in vain that she
endeavoured at first to deceive herself; her
feelings were witnesses too acute of it's
reality; with as little success did she try to
sleep it off, for the pain she suffered prevented her closing her Eyes—. She then
summoned her Maid and with the Assistance
of

of the Housekeeper, every remedy that the receipt book or the head of the latter contained, was tried, but ineffectually; for though for a short time releived by them, the pain still returned. She was now obliged to give up the endeavour, and to reconcile herself not only to the pain of a Toothake, but to the loss of a Ball; and though she had with so much eagerness looked forward to the day of its arrival, had received such pleasure in the necessary preparations, and promised herself so much delight in it, Yet she was not so totally void of philosophy as many Girls of her age, might have been in her situation. She considered that there were Misfortunes of a much greater magnitude than the loss of a Ball, experienced every day by some part of Mortality, and that the time might come when She would herself look back with Wonder and perhaps with Envy on her having known no greater vexation. By such reflections as these, she soon reasoned herself into as much Resignation & Patience as the pain she suffered, would allow of, which after

after all was the greatest Misfortune of the two, and told the sad story when she entered the Breakfast room, with tolerable Composure. M^rs Percival more grieved for her toothake than her Disappointment, as she feared that it would not be possible to prevent her Dancing with a *Man* if she went, was eager to try everything that had already been applied to alleviate the pain, while at the same time She declared it was impossible for her to leave the House. Miss Stanley who joined to her concern for her Freind, felt a mixture of Dread lest her Mother's proposal that they should all remain at home, might be accepted, was very violent in her sorrow on the occasion, and though her apprehensions on the subject were soon quieted by Kitty's protesting that sooner than allow any one to stay with her, she would herself go, she continued to lament it with such unceasing vehemence as at last drove Kitty to her own room. Her Fears for herself being now entirely dissipated left her more than ever at leisure to pity and persecute

persecute her Freind who tho' safe when in her own room, was frequently removing from it to some other in hopes of being more free from pain, and then had no opportunity of escaping her—.

"To be sure, there never was anything so shocking, said Camilla; To come on such a day too! For one would not have minded it you know had it been at *any other* time. But it always is so. I never was at a Ball in my Life, but what something happened to prevent somebody from going! I wish there were no such things as Teeth in the World; they are nothing but plagues to one, and I dare say that People might easily invent something to eat with instead of them; Poor Thing! what pain you are in! I declare it is quite Shocking to look at you. But you wo'nt have it out, will you? For Heaven's sake do'nt; for there is nothing I dread so much. I declare I had rather undergo the greatest Tortures in the World than have a tooth drawn. Well! how patiently you do bear it! how can you be so quiet? Lord, if I were in your place I should make such a fuss, there would be no bearing me. I should torment you to Death."

"So you do, as it is," thought Kitty.

"For my own part, Catherine said M^{rs} Percival I have not a doubt but that you caught this toothake by sitting so much in that Arbour, for it is always damp. I know it has ruined your Constitution entirely; and indeed I do not beleive it has been of much service to mine; I sate down in it last May to rest myself, and I have never been quite well since—. I shall order John to pull it all down I assure you."

"I know you will not do that Ma'am, said Kitty, as you must be convinced how unhappy it would make me."

"You talk very ridiculously Child; it is all whim & Nonsense. Why cannot you fancy this room an Arbour?

"Had this room been built by Cecilia & Mary, I should have valued it equally Ma'am, for it is not merely the name of an Arbour, which charms me."

"Why

"Why indeed M^rs Percival, said M^rs Stanley, I must think that Catherine's affection for her Bower is the effect of a Sensibility that does her Credit. I love to see a Freindship between young Persons[1] and always consider it as a sure mark of an aimiable affectionate disposition.[2] I have from Camilla's infancy taught her to think the same, and have taken great pains to introduce her to young people of her own age who were likely to be worthy of her regard. [There is something mighty pretty I think in young Ladies corresponding with each other, and][3] nothing forms the taste more than sensible & Elegant Letters—. Lady Halifax thinks just like me—. Camilla corresponds with her Daughters, and I beleive I may venture to say that they are none of them *the worse* for it." These ideas were too modern to suit M^rs Percival who considered a correspondence between Girls

---

[1] ladies *erased*.
[2] of their being disposed to like one another *erased*.
[3] *Erased*.

as

as productive of no good, and as the frequent origin of imprudence & Error by the
effect of pernicious advice and bad Example.
She could not therefore refrain from saying
that for her part, she had lived fifty Years
in the world without having ever had a
correspondent, and did not find herself at
all the less respectable for it—. Mʳˢ Stanley
could say nothing in answer to this, but her
Daughter who was less governed by Propriety, said in her thoughtless way, "But
who knows what you might have been
Ma'am, if you *had* had a Correspondent;
perhaps it would have made you quite a
different Creature. I declare I would not
be without those I have for all the World.
It is the greatest delight of my Life, and
you cannot think how much their Letters
have formed my taste as Mama says, for
I hear from them generally every week."

"You received a Letter from Augusta
Barlow to day, did not you my Love? said
her Mother—. She writes remarkably well
I know.'

"Oh!

"Oh! Yes Ma'am, the most delightful
Letter you ever heard of. She sends me a long
account of the new Regency walking dress[1]
Lady Susan has given her, and it is so beautiful that I am quite dieing with envy for it."

"Well, I am prodigiously happy to hear
such pleasing news of my young freind; I
have a high regard for Augusta, and most
sincerely partake in the general Joy on the
occasion. But does she say nothing else?
it seemed to be a long Letter—Are they to
be at Scarborough?"

"Oh! Lord, she never once mentions it,
now I recollect it; and I entirely forgot to
ask her when I wrote last. She says nothing
indeed except about the Regency."[2] "She
*must* write well thought Kitty, to make a
long Letter upon a Bonnet & Pelisse."[3]
She then left the room tired of listening to
a conversation which tho' it might have
diverted her had she been well, served only
to fatigue and depress her, while in pain.

---

[1] R w d *over* Bonnet *erased.*     [2] Bonnet *erased.*
[3] Jacket and petticoat *erased.*

Happy

Happy was it for *her*, when the hour of dressing came, for Camilla satisfied with being surrounded by her Mother and half the Maids in the House did not want her assistance, and was too agreably employed to want her Society. She remained therefore alone in the parlour, till joined by M^r Stanley & her Aunt, who however after a few enquiries, allowed her to continue[1] undisturbed and began their usual conversation on Politics. This was a subject on which they could never agree, for M^r Stanley who considered himself as perfectly qualified by his Seat in the House, to decide on it without hesitation, resolutely maintained that the Kingdom had not for ages been in so flourishing & prosperous a state, and M^rs Percival with equal warmth, tho' perhaps less argument, as vehemently asserted that the whole Nation would speedily be ruined, and everything as she expressed herself be at sixes & sevens. It was not however unamusing to Kitty to listen to the

[1] remain *erased*.

Dispute

Dispute, especially as she began then to be more free from pain, and without taking any share in it herself, she found it very entertaining to observe the eagerness with which they both defended their opinions, and could not help thinking that M$^r$ Stanley would not feel more disappointed if her Aunt's expectations were fulfilled, than her Aunt would be mortified by their failure. After waiting a considerable time M$^{rs}$ Stanley & her daughter appeared, and Camilla in high Spirits, & perfect good humour with her own looks, was more violent than ever in her lamentations over her Freind as she practised her scotch Steps about the room—. At length they departed, & Kitty better able to amuse herself than she had been the whole Day before, wrote a long account of her Misfortunes to Mary Wynne. When her Letter was concluded she had an opportunity of witnessing the truth of that assertion which says that Sorrows are lightened by Communication, for her toothake was then so much releived that

that she began to entertain an idea of following her Freinds to Mʳ Dudley's. They had
been gone an hour,[1] and as every thing
relative to her Dress was in complete
readiness, She considered that in another
hour[2] since there was so little a way to go,
She might be there—. They were gone in
Mʳ Stanley's Carriage and therefore She
might follow in her Aunt's. As the plan
seemed so very easy to be executed, and
promising so much pleasure,[3] it was after
a few Minutes deliberation finally adopted,
and running up stairs, She rang in great
haste for her Maid. The Bustle & Hurry
which then ensued for nearly an hour was
at last happily concluded by her finding
herself very well-dressed and in high Beauty.
Anne[4] was then dispatched in the same haste
to order the Carriage, while her Mistress was
putting on her gloves, & arranging the folds
of her dress, [and providing herself with

[1] but half *erased before* an hour
[2] an hour & a half *erased.*
[3] in itself *erased after* pleasure.
[4] Nanny *erased.*

Lavender

Lavender water][1]. In a few Minutes she heard the Carriage drive up to the Door, and tho' at first surprised at the expedition with which it had been got ready, she concluded after a little reflection that the Men had received some hint of her intentions beforehand, and was hastening out of the room, when Anne came running into it in the greatest hurry and agitation, exclaiming "Lord Ma'am! Here's a Gentleman in a Chaise and four come, and I cannot for my Life conceive who it is! I happened to be crossing the hall when the Carriage drove up, and I knew nobody would be in the way to let him but Tom, and he looks so awkward you know Ma'am, now his hair is just done up, that I was not willing the gentleman should see him, and so I went to the door myself. And he is one of the handsomest young Men you would wish to see; I was almost ashamed of being seen in my Apron Ma'am,[2]

[1] *Erased.*
[2] in my Apron Ma'am *for* because you know Ma'am I am all over powder *erased.*

but

but however he is vastly handsome and did not seem to mind it at all.—And he asked me whether the Family were at home; and so I said everybody was gone out but you Ma'am, for I would not deny you because I was sure you would like to see him. And then he asked me whether M^r and M^rs Stanley were not here, and so I said Yes, and then——

"Good Heavens! said Kitty, what can all this mean! And who can it possibly be! Did you never see him before? And Did not he tell you his Name?"

"No Ma'am, he never said anything about it—So then I asked him to walk into the parlour, and he was prodigious agreable, and——

"Whoever he is, said her Mistress, he has made a great impression upon you Nanny—But where did he come from? and what does he want here?

"Oh! Ma'am, I was going to tell you, that I fancy his business is with you; for he asked me whether you were at leisure to see any-body

body, and desired I would give his Compli-
ments to you, & say he should be very happy
to wait on you—However I thought he had
better not come up into your Dressing room,
especially as everything is in such a litter,
so I told him if he would be so obliging as
to stay in the parlour, I would run up stairs
and tell you he was come, and I dared to
say that you would wait upon *him*. Lord
Ma'am, I'd lay anything that he is come to
ask you to dance with him tonight, & has
got his Chaise ready to take you to Mr.
Dudley's."

Kitty could not help laughing at this
idea, & only wished it might be true, as it
was very likely that she would be too late
for any other partner—"But what, in the
name of wonder, can he have to say to me?
Perhaps he is come to rob the house—he
comes in stile at least; and it will be some
consolation for our losses to be robbed by a
Gentleman in a Chaise & 4—. What Livery
has his Servants?"

"Why that is the most wonderful thing
about

about him Ma'am, for he has not a single
servant with him, and came with hack
horses; But he is as handsome as a Prince
for all that, and has quite the look of one.
Do dear Ma'am, go down, for I am sure you
will be delighted with him—"

"Well, I beleive I must go; but it is very
odd! What can he have to say to me."
Then giving one look at herself in the Glass,
she walked with great impatience, tho'
trembling all the while from not knowing
what to expect, down Stairs, and after
pausing a moment at the door to gather
Courage for opening it, she resolutely
entered the room. The Stranger, whose
appearance did not disgrace the account she
had received of it from her Maid, rose up on
her entrance, and laying aside the Newspaper
he had been reading, advanced towards her
with an air of the most perfect Ease &
Vivacity, and said to her, "It is certainly
a very awkward circumstance to be thus
obliged to introduce myself, but I trust that
the necessity of the case will plead my
Excuse

Excuse, and prevent your being prejudiced
by it against me—. *Your* name, I need not
ask Ma'am—. Miss Percival is too well
known to me by description to need any
information of that." Kitty, who had been
expecting him to tell his own name, instead
of hers, and who from having been little in
company, and never before in such a situation, felt herself unable to ask it, tho' she
had been planning her speech all the way
down stairs, was so confused & distressed
by this unexpected address that she could
only return a slight curtesy to it, and
accepted the chair he reached her, without
knowing what she did. The gentleman then
continued. "You are, I dare say, surprised
to see me returned from France so soon, and
nothing indeed but business could have
brought me to England; a very Melancholy
affair has now occasioned it, and I was
unwilling to leave it without paying my
respects to the Family in Devonshire whom
I have so long wished to be acquainted
with—." Kitty, who felt much more surprised
at

at his supposing her *to be so*, than at seeing
a person in England, whose having ever left
it was perfectly unknown to her, still continued silent from Wonder & Perplexity,
and her visitor still continued to talk. "You
will suppose Madam that I was not the *less*
desirous of waiting on you, from your having
M^r & M^rs Stanley with you—. I hope they
are well? And M^rs Percival how does *she*
do?" Then without waiting for an answer
he gaily added, "But my dear Miss Percival
you are going out I am sure; and I am
detaining you from your appointment. How
can I ever expect to be forgiven for such
injustice! Yet how can I, so circumstanced,
forbear to offend! You seem dressed for a
Ball? But this is the Land of gaiety I
know; I have for many years been desirous
of visiting it. You have Dances I suppose
at least every week—But where are the rest
of your party gone, and what kind Angel
in compassion to me, has excluded *you*
from it?"

"Perhaps Sir, said Kitty extremely confused

fused by his manner of speaking to her, and highly displeased with the freedom of his Conversation towards one who had never seen him before and did not *now* know his name, "perhaps Sir, you are acquainted with M^r & M^rs Stanley; and your business may be with *them*?"

"You do me too much honour Ma'am, replied he laughing, in supposing me to be acquainted with M^r & M^rs Stanley; I merely know them by sight; very distant relations; only my Father & Mother. Nothing more I assure you."

"Gracious Heaven! said Kitty, are *you* M^r Stanley then?—I beg a thousand pardons—Though really upon recollection I do not know for what—for you never told me your name——"

"I beg your pardon—I made a very fine speech when you entered the room, all about introducing myself; I assure you it was very great for *me*."

"The speech had certainly great Merit, said Kitty smiling; I thought so at the time;
but

but since you never mentioned your name in it, as an *introductory one* it might have been better."

There was such an air of good humour and Gaiety in Stanley, that Kitty, tho' perhaps not authorized to address him with so much familiarity on so short an acquaintance, could not forbear indulging the natural Unreserve & Vivacity of her own Disposition, in speaking to him, as he spoke to her. She was intimately acquainted too with his Family who were her relations, and she chose to consider herself entitled by the connexion to forget how little a while they had known each other. "M^r & M^rs Stanley and your Sister are extremely well, said she, and will I dare say be very much surprised to see you—But I am sorry to hear that your return to England has been occasioned by any unpleasant circumstance."

"Oh! Do'nt talk of it, said he, it is a most confounded shocking affair, & makes me miserable to think of it; But where are my Father & Mother, & your Aunt gone? Oh!
Do

Do you know that I met the prettiest little waiting maid in the world, when I came here; she let me into the house; I took her for you at first."

"You did me a great deal of honour, and give me more credit for good nature than I deserve, for I *never* go to the door when any one comes."

"Nay do not be angry; I mean no offence. But tell me, where are you going to so smart? Your carriage is just coming round."

"I am going to a Dance at a Neighbour's[1], where your Family and my Aunt are already gone."

"Gone, without you! what's the meaning of *that*? But I suppose you are like myself, rather long in dressing."

"I must have been so indeed, if that were the case for they have been gone nearly these two hours; The reason however was not what you suppose—I was prevented going by a pain——

"By a pain! interrupted Stanley, Oh!

[1] of ours *erased*.

heavens,

heavens, that is dreadful indeed! No Matter where the pain was. But my dear Miss Percival, what do you say to my accompanying you? And suppose you were to dance with me too? *I* think it would be very pleasant."

"I can have no objection to either I am sure, said Kitty laughing to find how near the truth her Maid's conjecture had been; on the contrary I shall be highly honoured by both, and I can answer for Your being extremely welcome to the Family who give the Ball."

"Oh! hang them; who cares for that; they cannot turn me out of the house. But I am afraid I shall cut a sad figure among all your Devonshire Beaux in this dusty, travelling apparel, and I have not wherewithal to change it. You can procure[1] me some powder perhaps, and I must get a pair of Shoes from one of the Men, for I was in such a devil of a hurry to leave Lyons that I had not time to have anything pack'd up[2] but some linen." Kitty very readily undertook

---

[1] lend *erased*.    [2] pack up anything *erased*.

to procure for him everything he wanted, &
telling the footman to shew him into M<sup>r</sup>
Stanley's dressing room, gave Nanny orders
to send in some powder & pomatum, which
orders Nanny chose to execute in person.
As Stanley's preparations in dressing were
confined to such very trifling articles, Kitty
of course expected him in about ten minutes;
but she found that it had not been merely a
boast of vanity in saying that he was dilatory
in that respect, as he kept her waiting for
him above half an hour, so that the Clock
had struck ten before he entered the room
and the rest of the party had gone by eight.

"Well, said he as he came in, have not I
been very quick? I never hurried so much
in my Life before."

"In that case you certainly have, replied
Kitty, for all Merit you know is com-
parative."

"Oh! I knew you would be delighted with
me for making so must¹ haste—. But come,
the Carriage is ready; so, do not keep me

¹ *sic.*

waiting

waiting." And so saying he took her by the hand, & led her out of the room. "Why, my dear Cousin, said he when they were seated, this will be a most agreable surprize to everybody to see you enter the room with such a smart Young Fellow as I am—I hope your Aunt won't be alarmed."

"To tell you the truth, replied Kitty, I think the best way to prevent it, will be to send for her, or your Mother before we go into the room, especially as you are a perfect stranger, & must of course be introduced to M^r & M^rs Dudley—"

"Oh! Nonsense, said he; I did not expect *you* to stand upon such Ceremony; Our acquaintance with each other renders all such Prudery, ridiculous; Besides, if we go in together, we shall be the whole talk of the Country—"

"To *me* replied Kitty, that would certainly be a most powerful inducement; but I scarcely know whether my Aunt would consider it as such—. Women at her time of life, have odd ideas of propriety you know."

"Which

"Which is the very thing that you ought to break them of; and why should you object to entering a room with me where all our relations are, when you have done me the honour to admit me without any chaprone into your Carriage? Do not you think your Aunt will be as much offended with you for one, as for the other of these mighty crimes."

"Why really said Catherine, I do not know but that she may; however, it is no reason that I should offend against Decorum a second time, because I have already done it once."

"On the contrary, that is the very reason which makes it impossible for you to prevent it, since you cannot offend for the *first time* again."

"You are very ridiculous, said she laughing, but I am afraid your arguments divert me too much to convince me."

"At least they will convince you that I am very agreable, which after all, is the happiest conviction for me, and as to the affair of Propriety we will let that rest till we

we arrive at our Journey's end—. This is
a monthly Ball I suppose. Nothing but
Dancing here—."

"I thought I had told you that it was
given by a M^r Dudley—"

"Oh! aye so you did; but why should not
M^r Dudley give one every month? By the
bye who *is that* Man? Everybody gives
Balls now I think; I beleive I must give one
myself soon—. Well, but how do you like
my Father & Mother? And poor little
Camilla too, has not she plagued you to
death with the Halifaxes?" Here the
Carriage fortunately stopped at M^r Dudley's,
and Stanley was too much engaged in
handing her out of it, to wait for an answer,
or to remember that what he had said
required one. They entered the small
vestibule which M^r Dudley had raised to the
Dignity of a Hall, & Kitty immediately
desired the footman who was leading the
way upstairs, to inform either M^rs Peterson,
or M^rs Stanley of her arrival, & beg them
to come to her, but Stanley unused to any
contradiction

contradiction & impatient to be amongst
them, would neither allow her to wait, or
listen to what she said, & forcibly seizing her
arm within his, overpowered her voice with
the rapidity of his own, & Kitty half angry,
& half laughing was obliged to go with
him up stairs, and could even with difficulty
prevail on him to relinquish her hand before
they entered the room. M^rs Percival was at
that very moment engaged in conversation
with a Lady at the upper end of the room,
to whom she had been giving a long account
of her Neice's unlucky disappointment, &
the dreadful pain that she had with so much
fortitude, endured the whole Day—"I left
her however, said she, thank heaven!, a little
better, and I hope she has been able to
amuse herself with a book, poor thing! for
she must otherwise be very dull. She is
probably in bed by this time, which while
she is so poorly, is the best place for her you
know Ma'am." The Lady was going to give
her assent to this opinion, when the Noise
of voices on the stairs, and the footman's
opening

opening the door as if for the entrance of
Company, attracted the attention of every
body in the room; and as it was in one of
those Intervals between the Dances when
every one seemed glad to sit down, M^{rs}
Peterson had a most unfortunate opportunity of seeing her Neice whom she had
supposed in bed, or amusing herself as the
height of gaity with a book, enter the room
most elegantly dressed, with a smile on her
Countenance, and a glow of mingled Chearfulness & Confusion on her Cheeks, attended
by a young Man uncommonly handsome,
and who without any of her Confusion,
appeared to have all her vivacity. M^{rs}
Percival colouring with anger & astonishment, rose from her Seat, & Kitty walked
eagerly towards her, impatient to account
for what she saw appeared wonderful to
every body, and extremely offensive to *her*,
while Camilla on seeing her Brother ran
instantly towards him, and very soon
explained who he was by her words & her
actions. M^{r} Stanley, who so fondly doated

on

on his Son, that the pleasure of seeing him
again after an absence of three Months
prevented his feeling for the time any anger
against him for returning to England without his knowledge, received him with equal
surprise & delight; and soon comprehending
the cause of his Journey, forbore any further
conversation with him, as he was eager to
see his Mother, & it was necessary that he
should be introduced to M^r Dudley's family.
This introduction to any one but Stanley
would have been highly unpleasant, for they
considered their dignity injured by his
coming uninvited to their house, & received
him with more than their usual haughtiness:
But Stanley who with[1] a vivacity of temper
seldom subdued, & a contempt of censure
not to be overcome, possessed an opinion of
his own Consequence, & a perseverance in
his own schemes which were not to be
damped by the conduct of others, appeared
not to perceive it. The Civilities therefore
which they coldly offered, he received with

---

[1] joined to *erased.*

a

a gaiety & ease peculiar to himself, and then attended by his Father & Sister walked into another room where his Mother was playing at Cards, to experience another Meeting, and undergo a repetition of pleasure, surprise, & Explanations. While these were passing, Camilla eager to communicate all she felt to some one who would attend to her, returned to Catherine, & seating herself by her, immediately began—"Well, did you ever know anything so delightful as this? But it always is so; I never go to a Ball in my Life but what something or other happens unexpectedly that is quite charming!"

"A Ball replied Kitty, seems to be a most eventful thing to you—"

"Oh! Lord, it is indeed—But only think of my brother's returning so suddenly— And how shocking a thing it is that has brought him over! I never heard anything so dreadful—!"

"What is it pray that has occasioned his leaving France? I am sorry to find that it is a melancholy event."

"Oh!

"Oh! it is beyond anything you can conceive! His favourite Hunter who was turned out in the park on his going abroad, somehow or other fell ill—No, I beleive it was an accident, but however it was something or other, or else it was something else, and so they sent an Express immediately to Lyons where my Brother was, for they knew that he valued this Mare more than anything else in the World besides; and so my Brother set off directly for England, and without packing up another Coat; I am quite angry with him about it; it was so shocking you know to come away without a change of Cloathes—"

"Why indeed said Kitty, it seems to have been a very shocking affair from beginning to end."

"Oh! it is beyond anything You can conceive! I would rather have had *anything* happen than that he should have lossed that mare."

"Except his[1] coming away without another coat."

[1] your Brother's *erased.*

"Oh!

"Oh! yes, that has vexed me more than you can imagine—. Well, & so Edward got to Brampton just as the poor Thing was dead; but as he could not bear to remain there *then*, he came off directly to Chetwynde on purpose to see us—. I hope he may not go abroad again."

"Do you think he will not?"

"Oh! dear, to be sure he must, but I wish he may not with all my heart—. You cannot think how fond I am of him! By the bye are not you in love with him yourself?"

"To be sure I am replied Kitty laughing, I am in love with every handsome Man I see."

"That is just like me—*I* am always in love with every handsome Man in the World."

"There you outdo me replied Catherine for I am only in love with those I *do* see."

M^rs Percival who was sitting on the other side of her, & who began now to distinguish the words, *Love* & *handsome Man*, turned hastily towards them, & said "What are you

you talking of Catherine?" To which
Catherine immediately answered with the
simple artifice of a Child, "Nothing Ma'am."
She had already received a very severe
lecture from her Aunt on the imprudence
of her behaviour during the whole evening;
She blamed her for coming to the Ball, for
coming in the same Carriage with Edward
Stanley, and still more for entering the
room with him. For the last-mentioned
offence Catherine knew not what apology
to give, and tho' she longed in answer to
the second to say that she had not thought
it would be civil to make M$^r$ Stanley *walk*,
she dared not so to trifle with her aunt, who
would have been but the more offended by
it. The first accusation however she considered as very unreasonable, as she thought
herself perfectly justified in coming. This
conversation continued till Edward Stanley
entering the room came instantly towards
her, and telling her that every one waited
for *her* to begin the next Dance led her to
the top of the room, for Kitty impatient to
escape

escape from so unpleasant a Companion, without the least hesitation, or one civil scruple at being so distinguished, immediately gave him her hand, & joyfully left her seat. This Conduct however was highly resented by several young Ladies present, and among the rest by Miss Stanley whose regard for her brother tho' *excessive*, & whose affection for Kitty tho' *prodigious*, were not proof against such an injury to her importance and her peace. Edward had however only consulted his own inclinations in desiring Miss Peterson to begin the Dance, nor had he any reason to know that it was either wished or expected by anyone else in the Party. As an heiress she was certainly of consequence, but her Birth gave her no other claim to it, for her Father had been a Merchant. It was this very circumstance which rendered this unfortunate affair so offensive to Camilla, for tho' she would sometimes boast in the pride of her heart, & her eagerness to be admired that she did not know who her grandfather had been, and

was

was as ignorant of everything relative to
Genealogy as to Astronomy, (and she might
have added, Geography) yet she was really
proud of her family & Connexions, and
easily offended if they were treated with
Neglect. "I should not have minded it, said
she to her Mother, if she had been *anybody*
else's daughter; but to see her pretend to be
above *me*, when her Father was only a
tradesman, is too bad! It is such an affront
to our whole Family! I declare I think Papa
ought to interfere in it, but he never cares
about anything but Politics. If I were
M^r Pitt or the Lord Chancellor, he would
take care I should not be insulted, but he
never thinks about *me*; And it is so provok-
ing that *Edward* should let her stand there.
I wish with all my heart that he had never
come to England! I hope she may fall down
& break her neck, or sprain her Ancle."
M^rs Stanley perfectly agreed with her
daughter concerning the affair, & tho' with
less violence, expressed almost equal resent-
ment at the indignity. Kitty in the mean-
time

time remained insensible of having given any one Offence, and therefore unable either to offer an apology, or make a reparation; her whole attention was occupied by the happiness she enjoyed in dancing with the most elegant young Man in the room, and every one else was equally unregarded. The Evening indeed to *her*, passed off delightfully; he was her partner during the greatest part of it, and the united attractions that he possessed of Person, Address & vivacity, had easily gained that preference from Kitty which they seldom fail of obtaining from every one. She was too happy to care either for her Aunt's illhumour which she could not help remarking,[1] or for the Alteration in Camilla's behaviour which forced itself at last on her observation. Her Spirits were elevated above the influence of Displeasure in any one, and she was equally indifferent as to the cause of Camilla's, or the continuance of her Aunt's. Though Mr Stanley could never be really offended by any im-

[1] observing *erased*.

prudence

prudence or folly in his Son[1] that had given
him the pleasure of seeing him,[2] he was yet
perfectly convinced that Edward ought not
to remain in England, and was resolved to
hasten his leaving it as soon as possible; but
when he talked to Edward about it, he found
him much less disposed towards returning
to France, than to accompany them in their
projected tour, which he assured his Father
would be infinitely more pleasant to him,
and that as to the affair of travelling he considered it of no importance, and what might
be pursued at any little odd time, when he
had nothing better to do. He advanced
these objections in a manner which plainly
shewed that he had scarcely a doubt of their
being complied with, and appeared to consider his father's arguments in opposition to
them, as merely given with a veiw to keep
up his authority, & such as he should find
little difficulty in combating. He concluded
at last by saying, as the chaise in which they

[1] in his Son *added above line.*
[2] his *erased.*

5302                   H                   returned

returned together from M^r Dudley's reached
M^rs Percivals, "Well Sir, we will settle this
point some other time, and fortunately it is
of so little consequence, that an immediate
discussion of it is unnecessary." He then got
out of the chaise & entered the house without
waiting for his Father's reply. It was not till
their return that Kitty could account for that
coldness in Camilla's behaviour to her, which
had been so pointed as to render it impossible
to be entirely unnoticed. When however
they were seated in the Coach with the two
other Ladies, Miss Stanley's indignation was
no longer to be suppressed from breaking
out into words, & found the following vent.

"Well, I must say *this*, that I never was at
a stupider Ball in my Life! But it always is
so; I am always disappointed in them for
some reason or other. I wish there were no
such things."

"I am sorry Miss Stanley, said M^rs Percival
drawing herself up, that you have not been
amused; every thing was meant for the best
I am sure, and it is a poor encouragement
                                        for

for your Mama to take you to another if you
are so hard to be satisfied."

"I do not know what you mean Ma'am
about Mama's *taking* me to another. You
know I am come out."

"Oh! dear M^rs Percival, said M^rs Stanley,
you must not beleive everything that my
lively Camilla says, for her spirits are prodigiously high sometimes, and she frequently
speaks without thinking. I am sure it is
impossible for *any one* to have been at a
more elegant or agreable dance, and so she
wishes to express herself I am certain."

"To be sure I do, said Camilla very
sulkily, only I must say that it is not very
pleasant to have any body behave so rude
to me as to be quite shocking! I am sure
I am not at all offended, and should not care
if all the World were to stand above me, but
still it is extremely abominable, & what I
cannot put up with. It is not that I mind it
in the least, for I had just as soon stand at
the bottom as at the top all night long, if it
was not so very disagreable—. But to have a
person

person come in,[1] the middle of the Evening
& take everybody's place is what I am not
used to, and tho' I do not care a pin about
it myself, I assure you I shall not easily
forgive or forget it."

This speech which perfectly explained the
whole affair to Kitty, was shortly followed
on her side by a very submissive apology,
for she had too much good Sense to be proud
of her family, and too much good Nature to
live at variance with any one. The Excuses
she made, were delivered with so much real
concern for the Offence, and such unaffected
Sweetness, that it was almost impossible for
Camilla to retain that anger which had
occasioned them; She felt indeed most
highly gratified to find that no insult had
been intended and that Catherine was very
far from forgetting the difference in their
birth for which she could *now* only pity her,
and her good humour being restored with
the same Ease in which it had been affected,
she spoke with the highest delight of the

[1] *sic.*

Evening

Evening, & declared that she had never before been at so pleasant a Ball. The same endeavours that had procured the forgiveness of Miss Stanly ensured to her the cordiality of her Mother, and nothing was wanting but M^rs P's good humour to render the happiness of the others complete; but She, offended with Camilla for her affected Superiority, Still more so with her brother for coming to Chetwynde, & dissatisfied with the whole Evening, continued silent & Gloomy and was a restraint on the vivacity of her Companions. She eagerly seized the very first opportunity which the next Morning offered to her[1] of speaking to M^r Stanley on the subject of his son's return, and after having expressed her opinion of its being a very silly affair that he came at all, concluded with desiring him to inform M^r Edward Stanley that it was a rule with her never to admit a young Man into her house as a visitor for any length of time.

[1] offered *erased after* which; offered to her *added above line.*

"I

"I do not speak Sir, she continued, out of any disrespect to You, but I could not answer it to myself to allow of his stay; there is no knowing what might be the consequence of it, if he were to continue here, for girls nowadays will always give a handsome young Man the preference before any other, tho' for why, I never could discover, for what after all is Youth and Beauty? [Why in fact, it is nothing more than being Young and Handsome—and that][1] It is but a poor substitute for real worth & Merit; Beleive me Cousin that, what ever people may say to the contrary, there is certainly nothing like Virtue for making us what we ought to be, and as to a[2] young Man's, being young & handsome & having an agreable person, it is nothing at all to the purpose for he had much better be respectable. I always *did* think so, and I always *shall*, and therefore you will oblige me very much by desiring your son to leave Chetwynde, or I cannot be

---

[1] *erased, and* It *substituted.*
[2] handsome *erased after* a.

answerable

answerable for what may happen between
him and my Neice. You will be surprised to
hear *me* say it, she continued, lowering her
voice, but truth will out, and I must own
that Kitty is one of the most impudent Girls
that ever existed. [Her intimacies with
Young Men are abominable, and it is all the
same to her, who it is, no one comes amiss
to her][1] I assure you Sir, that I have seen
her sit and laugh and whisper with a young
Man whom she has not seen above half a
dozen times. Her behaviour indeed is
scandalous, and therefore I beg you will send
your Son away immediately, or everything
will be at sixes & sevens." Mr Stanley who
from one part of her Speech had scarcely
known to what length her insinuations of
Kitty's impudence were meant to extend,
now endeavoured to quiet her fears on the
occasion, by assuring her, that on every
account he meant to allow only of his son's
continuing that day with them, and that
she might depend on his being more earnest

[1] *Erased.*

in

in the affair from a wish of obliging her. He added also that he knew Edward to be very desirous himself of returning to France, as he wisely considered all time lost that did not forward the plans in which he was at present engaged, tho' he was but too well convinced of the contrary himself. His assurance in some degree quieted M<sup>rs</sup> P, & left her tolerably releived of her Cares & Alarms, & better disposed to behave with civility towards his Son during the short remainder of his stay at Chetwynde. M<sup>r</sup> Stanley went immediately to Edward, to whom he repeated the Conversation that had passed between M<sup>rs</sup> P & himself, & strongly pointed out the necessity of his leaving Chetwynde the next day, since his word was already engaged for it. His son however appeared struck only by the ridiculous apprehensions of M<sup>rs</sup> Peterson; and highly delighted at having occasioned them himself, seemed engrossed alone in thinking how he might encrease them, without attending to any other part of his Father's Conversation

versation. M^r Stanley could get no deter-
minate Answer from him, and tho' he still
hoped for the best, they parted almost in
anger on his side. His Son though by no
means disposed to marry, or any otherwise
attached to Miss Percival than as a good
natured lively Girl who seemed pleased with
him, took infinite pleasure in alarming the
jealous fears of her Aunt by his attentions
to her, without considering what effect they
might have on the Lady herself. He would
always sit by her when she was in the room,
appeared dissatisfied if she left it, and was
the first to enquire whether she meant soon
to return. He was delighted with her Drawings, and enchanted with her performance
on the Harpsichord; Everything that she
said, appeared to interest him; his Conversation was addressed to her alone, and
she seemed to be the sole object of his
attention. That such efforts should succeed
with one so tremblingly alive to every alarm
of the kind as M^rs Percival, is by no means
unnatural, and that they should have equal
influence

influence with her Neice whose imagination
was lively, and whose Disposition romantic,
who was already extremely pleased with him,
and of course desirous that he might be
so with her, is as little to be wondered at.
Every moment as it added to the conviction of his liking her, made him still more
pleasing, and strengthened in her Mind a wish
of knowing him better. As for M^rs Percival,
she was in tortures the whole Day; Nothing
that she had ever felt before on a similar
occasion was to be compared to the sensations
which then distracted her; her fears had
never been so strongly, or indeed so reason-
ably excited.[1]—Her dislike of Stanly, her
anger at her Neice, her impatience to have
them separated conquered every idea of propriety & Goodbreeding, and though he had
never mentioned any intention of leaving
them the next day, she could not help asking
him after Dinner, in her eagerness to have
him gone, at what time he meant to set out.

"Oh! Ma'am, replied he, if I am off by

[1] before *erased after* excited.

twelve

twelve at night, you may think yourself
lucky; and if I am not, you can only blame
yourself for having left so much as the *hour*
of my departure to my own disposal."
M^rs Percival coloured very highly at this
speech, and without addressing herself to
any one in particular, immediately began a
long harangue on the shocking behaviour of
modern young Men, & the wonderful Alteration that had taken place in them, since
her time, which she illustrated with many
instructive anecdotes of the Decorum &
Modesty which had marked the Characters
of those whom she had known, when she had
been young. This however did not prevent
his walking in the Garden with her Neice,
without any other companion for nearly an
hour in the course of the Evening. They had
left the room for that purpose with Camilla
at a time when M^rs Peterson had been out
of it, nor was it for some time after her
return to it, that she could discover where
they were. Camilla had taken two or three
turns with them in the walk which led to
the

the Arbour, but soon growing tired of listening to a Conversation in which she was seldom invited to join, & from its turning occasionally on Books, very little able to do it, she
left them together in the arbour,[1] to wander
alone to some other part of the Garden,
to eat the fruit, & examine M^{rs} Peterson's
Greenhouse. Her absence was so far from
being regretted, that it was scarcely noticed by
them, & they continued conversing together
on almost every subject, for Stanley seldom
dwelt long on any, and had something to say
on all, till they were interrupted by her Aunt.

Kitty was by this time perfectly convinced that both in Natural Abilities, &
acquired information, Edward Stanley was
infinitely superior to his Sister. Her desire
of knowing that he was so, had induced her
to take every opportunity of turning the
Conversation on History and they were very
soon engaged in an historical dispute, for
which no one was more calculated than
Stanley who was so far from being really

[1] together in the arbour *added above line.*

of

of any party, that he had scarcely a fixed
opinion on the Subject. He could therefore
always take either side, & always argue with
temper. In his indifference on all such topics
he was very unlike his Companion, whose
judgement being guided by her feelings
which were eager & warm, was easily
decided, and though it was not always
infallible, she defended it with a Spirit &
Enthuisasm[1] which marked her own reliance
on it. They had continued therefore for
sometime conversing in this manner on the
character of Richard the 3^d, which he was
warmly defending when he suddenly seized
hold of her hand, and exclaiming with great
emotion, "Upon my honour you are entirely
mistaken," pressed it passionately to his
lips, & ran out of the arbour. Astonished
at this behaviour, for which she was wholly
unable to account, she continued for a few
Moments motionless on the seat where he
had left her, and was then on the point of
following him up the narrow walk through

[1] *sic.*

which

which he had passed, when on looking up
the one that lay immediately before the
arbour, she saw her Aunt walking towards
her with more than her usual quickness.
This explained at once the reason of his
leaving her, but his leaving her in such
Manner was rendered still more inexplicable
by it. She felt a considerable degree of confusion at having been seen by her in such a
place with Edward, and at having that part
of his conduct, for which she could not herself account, witnessed by one to whom all
gallantry was odious. She remained therefore confused distressed & irresolute, and
suffered her Aunt to approach her, without
leaving the Arbour. M^{rs} Percival's looks
were by no means calculated to animate the
spirits of her Neice, who in silence awaited
her accusation, and in silence meditated her
Defence. After a few Moments suspence,
for M^{rs} Peterson was too much fatigued to
speak immediately, she began with great
Anger and Asperity, the following harangue.
"Well; *this* is beyond anything I could have
                                        supposed

supposed. *Profligate* as I *knew* you to be,
I was not prepared for such a sight. This is
beyond any thing you ever did *before*; beyond
any thing I ever heard of in my Life! Such
Impudence, I never witnessed before in such
a Girl! And this is the reward for all the
cares I have taken in your Education; for
all my troubles & Anxieties; and Heaven
knows how many they have been! All I
wished for, was to breed you up virtuously;
I never wanted you to play upon the Harpsichord, or draw better than any one else;
but I had hoped to see you respectable and
good; to see you able & willing to give
an example of Modesty and Virtue to the
Young people here abouts. I bought you
Blair's Sermons, and Cœlebs in Search of a
Wife,[1] I gave you the key to my own Library,
and borrowed a great many good books of
my Neighbours for you, all to this purpose.
But I might have spared myself the trouble
—Oh! Catherine, you are an abandoned

[1] Cœlebs *etc. substituted for* Seccar's explanation of
the Catechism. See note at end.

Creature

Creature, and I do not know what will become of you. I am glad however, she continued softening into some degree of Mildness, to see that you have some shame for what you have done, and if you are really sorry for it, and your future life is a life of penitence and reformation perhaps you may be forgiven. But I plainly see that every thing is going to sixes & sevens and all order will soon be at an end throughout the Kingdom."

"Not however Ma'am the sooner, I hope, from any conduct of mine, said Catherine in a tone of great humility, for upon my honour I have done nothing this evening that can contribute to overthrow the establishment of the kingdom."

"You are Mistaken Child, replied she; the welfare of every Nation depends upon the virtue of it's individuals, and any one who offends in so gross a manner against decorum & propriety is certainly hastening it's ruin. You have been giving a bad example to the World, and the World is but too well disposed to receive such."

"Pardon

"Pardon me Madam, said her Neice; but I *can* have given an Example only to *You*, for You alone have seen the offence. Upon my word however there is no danger to fear from what I have done; M^r Stanley's behaviour has given me as much surprise, as it has done to You, and I can only suppose that it was the effect of his high spirits, authorized in his opinion by our relationship. But do you consider Madam that it is growing very late? Indeed You had better return to the house." This speech as she well knew, would be unanswerable with her Aunt, who instantly rose, and hurried away under so many apprehensions for her own health, as banished for the time all anxiety about her Neice, who walked quietly by her side, revolving within her own Mind the occurrence that had given her Aunt so much alarm. "I am astonished at my own imprudence, said M^rs Percival; How could I be so forgetful as to sit down out of doors at such a time of night. I shall certainly have a return of my rheumatism after it—I begin

to feel very chill already. I must have
caught a dreadful cold by this time—I am
sure of being lain-up all the winter after it—"
Then reckoning with her fingers, "Let me
see; This is July; the cold weather will soon
be coming in—August—September—Octo-
ber — November — December — January
— February — March — April — Very likely
I may not be tolerable again before May.
I must and will have that arbour pulled
down—it will be the death of me; who
knows *now*, but what I may never recover—
Such things *have* happened—My particular
freind Miss Sarah Hutchinson's death was
occasioned by nothing more—She staid out
late one Evening in April, and got wet
through for it rained very hard, and never
changed her Cloathes when she came home—
It is unknown how many people have died
in consequence of catching Cold! I do not
beleive there is a disorder in the World
except the Smallpox which does not spring
from it." It was in vain that Kitty endeavoured to convince her that her fears on
                                        the

the occasion were groundless; that it was
not yet late enough to catch cold, and that
even if it were, she might hope to escape any
other complaint, and to recover in less than
ten Months. M^rs Percival only replied that
she hoped she knew more of Ill health than
to be convinced in such a point by a Girl
who had always been perfectly well, and
hurried up stairs leaving Kitty to make her
apologies to M^r & M^rs Stanley for going to
bed—. Tho' M^rs Percival seemed perfectly
satisfied with the goodness of the Apology
herself, yet Kitty felt somewhat embarrassed
to find that the only one she could offer to
their Visitors was that her Aunt had *perhaps*
caught cold, for M^rs Peterson charged her to
make light of it, for fear of alarming them.
M^r & M^rs Stanley however who well knew
that their Cousin was easily terrified on that
Score, received the account of it with very
little surprise, and all proper concern.
Edward & his Sister soon came in, & Kitty
had no difficulty in gaining an explanation
of his Conduct from him, for he was too
warm

warm on the subject himself, and too eager
to learn its success, to refrain from making
immediate Enquiries about it; & She could
not help feeling both surprised & offended
at the ease & Indifference with which he
owned that all his intentions had been to
frighten her Aunt by pretending an affection
for *her*, a design so very incompatible with
that partiality which she had at one time
been almost convinced of his feeling for her.
It is true that she had not yet seen enough
of him to be actually in love with him, yet
she felt greatly disappointed that so handsome, so elegant, so lively a young Man
should be so perfectly free from any such
Sentiment as to make it his principal Sport.
There was a Novelty in his character which
to *her* was extremely pleasing; his person
was uncommonly fine, his Spirits & Vivacity
suited to her own, and his Manners at once
so animated & insinuating, that she thought
it must be impossible for him to be otherwise than amiable, and was ready to give
him Credit for being perfectly[1] so. He

[1] completely *erased*.

knew

knew the powers of them himself; to them
he had often been endebted for his father's
forgiveness of faults which had he been
awkward & inelegant would have appeared
very serious; to them, even more than to
his person or his fortune, he owed the regard
which almost every one was disposed to feel
for him, and which Young Women in particular were inclined to entertain.[1] Their
influence was acknowledged on the present
occasion by Kitty, whose Anger they entirely
dispelled, and whose Chearfulness they had
power not only to restore, but to raise—.
The Evening passed off as agreably as the
one that had preceded it; they continued
talking to each other, during the cheif part
of it, and such was the power of his
Address, & the Brilliancy of his Eyes, that
when they parted for the Night, tho' Catherine had but a few hours before totally
given up the idea, yet she felt almost convinced again that he was really in love with
her. She reflected on their past Conversa-

[1] disposed to feel *erased*.

tion

tion, and tho' it had been on various & in-different subjects, and she could not exactly recollect any speech on his side expressive of such a partiality, she was still however nearly certain of it's being so; But fearful of being vain enough to suppose such a thing without sufficient reason, she resolved to suspend her final determination on it, till the next day, and more especially till their parting which she thought would infallibly explain his regard if any he had—. The more she had seen of him, the more inclined was she to like him, & the more desirous that he should like *her*. She was convinced of his being naturally very clever and very well disposed, and that his thoughtlessness & negligence, which tho' they appeared to *her* as very becoming in *him*, she was aware would by many people be considered as defects in his Character, merely proceeded from a vivacity always pleasing in Young Men, & were far from testifying a weak or vacant Understanding. Having settled this point within herself, and being perfectly convinced

convinced by her own arguments of it's
truth, she went to bed in high Spirits, determined to study his Character, and watch his
Behaviour still more the next day. She got
up with the same good resolutions and
would probably have put them in execution,
had not Anne informed her as soon as she
entered the room that M^r Edward Stanley
was already gone. At first she refused to
credit the information, but when her Maid
assured her that he had ordered a Carriage
the evening before to be there at seven
o'clock in the Morning and that she herself
had actually seen him depart in it a little
after eight, she could no longer deny her
beleif to it. "And this, thought she to herself blushing with anger at her own folly,
this is the affection for me of which I was so
certain. Oh! what a silly Thing is Woman!
How vain, how unreasonable! To suppose
that a young Man would be seriously
attached in the course of four & twenty
hours, to a Girl who has nothing to re-
commend her but a good pair of eyes! And
he

he is really gone! Gone perhaps without
bestowing a thought on me! Oh! why was
not I up by eight o'clock? But it is a proper
punishment for my Lazyness & Folly, and
I am heartily glad of it. I deserve it all, &
ten times more for such insufferable vanity.
It will at least be of service to me in that
respect; it will teach me in future *not* to
think Every Body is in love with me. Yet
I *should* like to have seen him before he
went, for perhaps it may be many Years
before we meet again. By his Manner of
leaving us however, he seems to have been
perfectly indifferent about it. How very
odd, that he should go without giving us
Notice of it, or taking leave of any one!
But it is just like a Young Man, governed
by the whim of the moment, or actuated
merely by the love of doing anything oddly!
Unaccountable Beings indeed! And Young
Women are equally ridiculous! I shall soon
begin to think like my Aunt that everything
is going to sixes & sevens, and that the whole
race of Mankind are degenerating." She
was

was just dressed, and on the point of leaving
her room to make her personal enquiries
after M^rs Peterson, when Miss Stanley
knocked at her door, & on her being
admitted began in her Usual Strain a long
harangue upon her Father's being so shocking as to make Edward go at all, and upon
Edward's being so horrid as to leave them
at such an hour in the Morning. "You have
no idea, said she, how surprised I was, when
he came into my Room to bid me good
bye—"

"Have you seen him then, this Morning?"
said Kitty.

"Oh Yes! And I was so sleepy that I
could not open my eyes. And so he said,
Camilla, goodbye to you for I am going
away—. I have not time to take leave of
any body else, and I dare not trust myself
to see Kitty, for then you know I should
never get away—"

"Nonsense, said Kitty; he did not say
that, or he was in joke if he did."

"Oh! no I assure you he was as much in
earnest

earnest as he ever was in his life; he was too much out of spirits to joke *then*. And he desired me when we all met at Breakfast to give his Comp<sup>ts</sup> to your Aunt, and his Love to you, for you was a nice Girl he said, and he only wished it were in his power to be more with You. You were just the Girl to suit him, because you were so lively and good-natured, and he wished with all his heart that you might not be married before he came back, for there was nothing he liked better than being here. Oh! you have no idea what fine things he said about you, till at last I fell asleep and he went away. But he certainly is in love with you—I am sure he is—I have thought so a great while I assure You."

"How can you be so ridiculous? said Kitty smiling with pleasure; I do not beleive him to be so easily affected. But he *did* desire his Love to me then? And wished I might not be married before his return? And said I was a Nice Girl, did he?"

"Oh! dear, Yes, and I assure You it is the

the greatest praise in his opinion, that he can bestow on any body; I can hardly ever persuade him to call *me* one, tho' I beg him sometimes for an hour together."

"And do You really think that he was sorry to go?"

"Oh! you can have no idea how wretched it made him. He would not have gone this Month, if my Father had not insisted on it; Edward told me so himself yesterday. He said that he wished with all his heart he had never promised to go abroad, for that he repented it more and more every day; that it interfered with all his other schemes, and that since Papa had spoken to him about it, he was more unwilling to leave Chetwynde than ever."

"Did he really say all this? And why would your father insist upon his going? "His leaving England interfered with all his other plans, and his Conversation with M^r Stanley had made him still more averse to it." What can this Mean?" "Why that he is excessively in love with you to be sure; what

what other plans can he have? And I suppose my father said that if he had not been going abroad, he should have wished him to marry you immediately.—But I must go and see your Aunt's plants—There is one of them that I quite doat on—and two or three more besides—"

"Can Camilla's explanation be true? said Catherine to herself, when her freind had left the room. And after all my doubts and Uncertainties, can Stanley really be averse to leaving England for *my sake* only? "His plans interrupted." And what indeed can his plans be, but towards Marriage? Yet *so soon* to be in love with me!—But it is the effect perhaps only of a warmth of heart which to *me* is the highest recommendation in any one. A Heart disposed to love—And such under the appearance of so much Gaity and Inattention, is Stanly's! Oh! how much does it endear him to me! But he is gone—Gone perhaps for Years—Obliged to tear himself from what he most loves, his happiness is sacrificed to the vanity of his Father! In

what

what anguish he must have left the house! Unable to see me, or to bid me adeiu, while I, senseless wretch, was daring to sleep. This, then explained his leaving us at such a time of day—. He could not trust himself to see me—. Charming Young Man! How much must you have suffered! I *knew* that it was impossible for one so elegant, and so well bred, to leave any Family in such a Manner, but for a Motive like this unanswerable." Satisfied, beyond the power of Change, of this, She went in high spirits to her Aunt's apartment, without giving a Moment's recollection on the vanity of Young Women, or the unaccountable conduct of Young Men.

Kitty continued in this state of satisfaction during the remainder of the Stanley's visit—Who took their leave with many pressing invitations to visit them in London, when as Camilla said, she might have an opportunity of becoming acquainted with that sweet girl Augusta Hallifax—Or[1] Rather

[1] Or *added above line.*

(thought

(thought Kitty,) of seeing my d<sup>r</sup> Mary Wynn again—M<sup>rs</sup> Percival in answer to M<sup>rs</sup> Stanley's invitation replied—That she looked upon London as the hot house of Vice where virtue had long been banished from Society & wickedness of every description was daily gaining ground—that Kitty was of herself sufficiently inclined to give way to, & indulge in vicious inclinations—& therefore was the last girl in the world to be trusted in London, as she would be totally unable to withstand temptation——

After the departure of the Stanleys Kitty returned to her usual occupations, but Alas! they had lost their power of pleasing. Her bower alone retained its interest in her feelings, & perhaps that was oweing to the particular remembrance it brought to her mind[1] of Ed<sup>wd</sup> Stanley.

The Summer passed away unmarked by any incident worth narrating, or any pleasure to Catharine save one, which arose from the reciept of a letter from her friend Cecilia now

[1] it brought to her mind *added above line.*

M<sup>rs</sup>

M$^{rs}$ Lascelles, announcing the speedy return
of herself & Husband to England.

A correspondance productive indeed of
little pleasure to either party had been
established between Camilla & Catharine.
The latter had now lost the only satisfaction
she had ever received from the letters of
Miss Stanley, as that young Lady having
informed her Friend of the departure of her
Brother to Lyons now never mentioned his
name—Her letters seldom contained any
Intelligence except a description[1] of some
new Article of Dress, an enumeration of
various engagements, a panegyric(?)[2] on
Augusta Halifax & perhaps a little abuse of
the unfortunate Sir Peter—

The Grove, for so was the Mansion of
M$^{rs}$ Percival at Chetwynde denominated was
situated w$^{h}$in five miles from Exeter,[3] but
though that Lady possessed a carriage &
horses of her [her] own, it was seldom that
Catharine could prevail on her to visit that

[1] the account *erased*.          [2] See note at end.
[3] the town *erased*.

town

town for the purpose of shopping, on account
of the many Officers perpetually Quartered
there & infested the principal Streets—A
company of strolling players in their way
from some Neighbouring Races having
opened a temporary Theatre there, M$^{rs}$
Percival was prevailed on by her Niece to
indulge her by attending the performance
once during their stay—M$^{rs}$ Percival insisted
on paying Miss Dudley the compliment of
inviting her to join the party, when a new
difficulty arose, from the necessity of having
some Gentleman to attend them[1]——

[1] to attend them *over* of their party *erased*.

*Here*

*Here follows a contribution to* Evelyn
*by Jane Austen's niece Anna Lefroy.*
*See the preface.*

On re entering his circular domain, his round-
Robin of perpetual peace; where enjoyment
had no end, and calamity no commencement,
his spirits became wonderfully composed,
and a delicious calm extended itself through
every nerve—With his pocket hankerchief
(once hemmed by the genius of the too
susceptible Rosa) he wiped the morbid
moisture from his brow;—then flew to the
Boudoir of his Maria—And, did *she* not fly
to meet her Frederick? Did she not dart
from the Couch on which she had so grace-
fully reclined, and, bounding like an agile
Fawn over the intervening Foot stool, pre-
cipitate herself into his arms? Does she not,
though fainting between every syllable,
breathe forth as it were by installments
her Frederick's adored name? Who is there
of perception so obtuse as not to realize the

K                        touching

touching scene? Who, of ear so dull as not
to catch the soft murmur of Maria's voice?
Ah! Who? The heart of every sympathetic
reader repeats, Ah, Who? Vain Echo!
Vain sympathy! There is no Meeting—no
Murmur—No Maria—It is not in the power
of language however potent; nor in that of
style, however diffuse to render justice to
the astonishment of M^r Gower—Arming
himself with a mahogany ruler which some
fatality had placed on Maria's writing table,
and calling repeatedly on her beloved Name,
he rushed forward to examine the adjacent
apartments—In the Dressing room of his lost
one he had the melancholy satisfaction of
picking up a curl paper, and a gust of wind,
as he re entered the Boudoir, swept from
the table, & placed at his feet a skein of
black sewing silk—These were the only
traces of Maria!! Carefully locking the doors
of these now desolate rooms, burying the
key deep in his Waistcoat pocket, & the
mystery of Maria's disappearance yet deeper
in his heart of hearts, M^r Gower left his once
happy

happy home, and sought a supper, and a Bed,
at the house of the hospitable M<sup>rs</sup> Willis—
There was an oppression on his chest which
made him extremely uncomfortable; he
regretted that instead of the skein of silk
carefully wrapped up in the curl paper &
placed beneath his pillow he had not rather
swallowed Laudanum—It would have been,
in all probability, more efficacious—At last,
M<sup>r</sup> Gower slept a troubled sleep, and in due
course of time he dreamt a troubled dream—
He dreamed of Maria, as how could he less?
She stood by his Bed side, in her Dressing
Gown—one hand held an open book, with
the forefinger of the other she pointed to this
ominous passage—"Tantôt c'est un vide;
qui nous ennuie; tantôt c'est un poids qui
nous oppresse"—The unfortunate Frederick
uttered a deep groan—& as the vision closed
the volume he observed these characters
strangely imprinted on the Cover—Rolandi
—Berners Street. *Who* was this dangerous
Rolandi? Doubtless a Bravo or a Monk—
possibly both—and what was he to Maria?
Vainly

Vainly he would have dared the worst, and put the fatal question—the semblance of Maria raised her monitory finger, and interdicted speech—Yet, some words she spoke, or seemed to speak her self; M^r Gower could distinguish only these—Search—Cupboard —Top shelf—Once more he essayed to speak, but it was all bewilderment—He heard strange Demon-like Sounds; hissing and spitting—he smelt an unearthly smell the agony became unbearable, and he awoke— Maria had vanished; the Rush light was expiring in the Socket; and the benevolent M^rs Willis entering his room, threw open the shutters, and in accordance with her own warmth of heart admitted the full blaze of a Summer morning's Sun—But what found he on reentering that circle of peace, that round Robin of perpetual peace

J. E. A. L.

# NOTES

*Page 27.* It will be remembered that poor Mrs. Smith, in *Persuasion*, aggravated Sir Walter's contempt by lodging in Westgate Buildings in Bath.

*Page 30.* Both 'The Beautiful Cassandra' (in Volume the First) and 'The History of England' (in Volume the Second) are dedicated to Miss Austen.

*Page 44.* Charlotte Smith published *Emmeline* 1788, *Ethelinde* 1790.

*Page 46.* Camilla's geography may remind us of Mrs. Bennet's idea of Newcastle, 'a place quite northward, it seems', or of Mrs. Musgrove's ignorance of the Bahamas.

*Page 109.* Had J. A. read Horace Walpole's *Historic Doubts* on the character of Richard III?

*Page 111.* Archbishop Secker's *Lectures on the Catechism of the Church of England* 1769. Blair's Sermons were admired by Mary Crawford. For *Cœlebs* see Letters 65, 66.

*Page 127.* The letters that end the word printed as *panegyric* are certainly not -*yric*; but that is probably Jane Austen's intention. This part of the manuscript is perhaps not in her hand, and it is possible that the writer copied mechanically an illegible word.

PRINTED IN
GREAT BRITAIN
AT THE
UNIVERSITY PRESS
OXFORD
BY
CHARLES BATEY
PRINTER
TO THE
UNIVERSITY